Believer on Tour

Young Believer™
ON TOUR

Paige

4

Stephen Arterburn
with Angela Hunt

TYNDALE KIDS

Tyndale House Publishers, Inc.
Wheaton, Illinois

Visit Tyndale's exciting Web site at www.tyndale.com

Visit the Young Believer Web site at www.youngbeliever.com

This novel is a work of fiction. Names, characters, places, and incidents are either the
product of the author's imagination or are used fictitiously. Any resemblance to actual
events, locales, organizations or persons, living or dead, is entirely coincidental and
beyond the intent of either the author or the publisher.

Library of Congress Cataloging-in-Publication Data

Arterburn, Stephen, date.
 Paige / Stephen Arterburn and Angela Elwell Hunt.
   p. cm. — (Young believer on tour ; 4)
 Summary: On the way to the float from which YB2 will be performing in Macy's
Thanksgiving Day Parade, Paige is separated from the other singers and kidnapped, but
with the help of God and a homeless woman, she might get free in time for the pop group's
television appearance.
 ISBN 0-8423-8338-7 (sc)
[1. Kidnapping—Fiction. 2. Blind—Fiction. 3. People with disabilities—Fiction.
4. Homeless persons—Fiction. 5. Parades—Fiction. 6. Musical groups—Fiction.
7. Christian life—Fiction.] I. Hunt, Angela Elwell, date. II. Title.
PZ7.A7435Pai 2004
[Fic]—dc22   2003024937

Printed in the United States of America

10   09   08   07   06   05   04
7   6   5   4   3   2   1

City street newsboy yells out the bad news,

CNN broadcasts grief, gloom, and despair,

People hunker down behind their closed doors,

Been so long since they have lifted a prayer,

God's still great and he is still on his throne,

Evil can never gain the upper hand,

If we call out we'll get a clear dial tone,

God's line is faster than the hottest broadband.

—Paige Clawson and Shane Clawson

FROM "COME ON (IT'S TIME TO TAKE YOUR STAND)"
YB2 MUSIC, INC.

November 15

YB2 DEBUTS IN HARTFORD

By Brooklyn Smith, the Hartford Register

"Welcome, Hartford, to the YB2 Never Stop Believin' Tour," Shane Clawson announced after taking the stage Saturday night. "Are you ready to go higher?"

And with that the band launched into "Go Vertical," a song currently riding the top of the pop charts. Whether you're into the teen scene or not, sales figures, polls, and the covers of teen magazines indicate that YB2 has already conquered a higher plane. The other young pop bands are struggling to keep up. Saturday night's appearance—the first for YB2 in Hartford—was even better than the concert I caught last year in Washington, DC. The band has matured, not only in age, but also in style. The vocalizations are more polished; the lyrics deeper than the bubblegum pop the group promoted last year. The group's moves are still tight, their friendship still evident. The teenage concert-goers got into the music and sang along with all the songs . . . when they weren't shrieking out the names of the group's resident heartthrobs.

YB2 leapt into the limelight two years ago when Ron Clawson formed the vocal group with his teenage offspring, Paige and Shane, then added newcomers Noah Dudash and Liane Nelson. This year he replaced singer Vance Gerkin with Josiah Johnson, a thirteen-year-old who packs a lot of punch in his pint-size frame.

The high-energy program kept the teens around me jumping up and down and singing along for nearly two and a half hours. During the break between the first and second sets, program director Ron Clawson made a striking choice—Paige Clawson and Noah Dudash performed a duet accompanied by keyboard and guitar—a quiet, moving tune that seemed to draw back the curtain on a teen's troubled soul. After all the celebration and joyous abandon of the first set, I was glad to see the singers acknowledge that pain exists in the world . . . and I was grateful they're willing to sing about it.

Songs like "Your Word" and "Just the Way That I Am" reveal

Paige

the group's Christian background, but tonight's show wasn't centered on religion—it was centered on music. Lively, hoppin' music.

The concert offered the ultimate in pop stargazing for fans who paid more than $60 for the majority of the convention center's 15,000 seats.

As the program wound down, some fans started moving toward the exits, but when the strains of YB2's monster hit "Y B Alone?" began to play, the teens halted in the aisles and the screaming began again.

I don't know if YB2 has what it takes to last ten years in this business—after all, these young singers have lives to begin, educations to pursue, careers to evaluate. Standing in the packed aisle, I wondered if they missed their families and friends back home.

But when I looked up at their images on the Jumbotron and saw the smiles on their faces, I thought, *Who wouldn't want to do that?*

If I were fourteen again, I'd sell my sister for the opportunity to be on that stage.

YB2. Long may they rock.

Paige groaned as the alarm clock buzzed from the bedside table. The air around her felt heavy, as did her arms. From the next bed she could hear the regular sounds of Liane's breathing.

"Hey, Lee." She fumbled to push herself up. "Can you reach the clock?"

"Hmflghpgh," Liane mumbled through her pillow, then Paige heard the sound of slapping. Finally, the clock fell silent and the room filled again with quiet.

They couldn't enjoy it, though. Today was Thanksgiving.

Paige sat up straighter and shook her head to clear the cobwebs from her brain. "What time is it?"

Silence. Then Liane sighed. "Six a.m. We'd better get moving."

"You want the bathroom first?"

"No. I want to sleep."

"You can't."

"I can dream, can't I?"

"As long as you don't go back to sleep."

Paige waited a minute, then threw back the covers and swung her feet off the bed. Liane would *have* to get up if Paige went through the room turning on the lights and the television. Though blindness prevented Paige from seeing the TV, she liked the noise, especially when they had a call time at 6:30 a.m.

Renewed groaning came from Liane's bed after Paige found the switch on the desk lamp. "Good grief, do you have to blind me?"

"Get up." Paige tapped her fingers over the desk in search of her hairbrush. She found it and began to pull the tangles from her short, soft hair. "You knew we'd be getting up early today, but you were so excited about this gig you talked until well after one o'clock last night—"

"All right, I'm up!"

Paige halted, listening, then she heard the sounds of Liane thumping across the floor. "I'm going to jump in the shower, okay? I'll be out in a sec, then the bathroom's all yours."

Paige nodded. "I'm going to check for messages."

Her searching fingers found her laptop right where she'd left it, so she lifted the lid and tapped the touch pad. A moment later the machine beeped to indicate she'd received at least one message during the night.

She touched the Enter key, which would highlight the

first message in the queue. Taz Trotter, YB2's soundman and technological genius, had equipped Paige's computer with a program that read her e-mails in a fairly realistic voice.

"Good morning, Paige," the male voice read, "don't forget to dress warmly under your black costume—though it's supposed to be sunny today, the forecast high is only twenty-four degrees. You girls can wear your coats down to the float, but you'll have to take them off when the parade starts. Okay? See you at the viewing stand. Break a leg. Dad."

Paige clicked the down arrow, but the little voice remained silent. Good—no more messages. She had enough to remember today. While the majority of American teenagers slept in on this holiday morning, she and her teammates would be shivering and singing in the Macy's Thanksgiving Day Parade.

She knew she ought to be excited . . . and she was. But couldn't they hold this parade later in the day—say, four o'clock?

They'd arrived in Manhattan late yesterday afternoon. While Larry Forsyth, their bus driver, took the bus to a parking garage, Paige and the other members of YB2 had hauled their luggage into the Mayflower Hotel across from Central Park.

Paige had stood in the center of the lobby, breathing in the scents of the building. "This place smells old," she'd said to no one in particular.

Noah had heard her, and laughed. "How can you tell?"

Paige lifted one shoulder in a shrug. "I dunno. New places smell like paint and carpet and cleaner. This place smells like wood and age and . . . dogs."

She had no sooner said the word than she heard barking.

"Do I hear dogs?" Noah asked the girl at the desk.

"We're one of the few hotels in Manhattan that accepts dogs," the girl answered. "Dogs that come to New York for the Westminster dog show stay with us."

It only made sense, Paige reasoned as she followed Liane to the elevator. Dogs would need to be across the street from a park, wouldn't they?

After checking in and unpacking, the group had gone out for a festive pre-Thanksgiving dinner, then they had taken a cab to an area between Central Park West and Columbus Avenue. RC, Paige's father and YB2's director, knew a network somebody who knew a Manhattan somebody who got them into a many-windowed room overlooking the area where volunteers inflated the huge parade balloons.

While her friends gasped in amazement, Paige had sat in a chair and tried to imagine what they were seeing. Taz was the most understanding—after watching for a few minutes, he stepped back from the window and tried to explain everything that was happening on the streets below.

"The people from Macy's call those inflatable things falloons," he said, "because they're part float, part balloon. They have to be filled the night before the parade."

"What are they filled with?" Paige asked.

"Helium, I think," Taz answered. "Though it must take an awful lot of the stuff to get those huge things up in the air."

"Oooooh, I know all about that," Liane said, butting into the conversation. "I was reading an article about the parade just yesterday. An average large falloon will weigh over four hundred pounds uninflated and can be up to forty feet tall when inflated. They hold over fifteen thousand cubic feet of helium, and sometimes it takes up to thirty people to guide the falloon as it moves down the parade route."

"Thank you, Miss Encyclopedia," Paige drawled.

Apparently not willing to be outdone in the parade trivia category, Taz cleared his throat. "I read they're all made in New Jersey and transported in trucks through the Lincoln Tunnel—so when they're packed they can't be any bigger than twelve and a half feet tall and eight feet wide."

"Well I read," Liane began again, "that in 1958 there was a helium shortage—"

Not in the mood for a history lesson, Paige interrupted her friend. "What kinds of falloons do you see out there?"

"Well—" she heard a smile in Taz's voice—"there's a huge peanut M&M with dangly arms and legs, a penguin, and a Spider-Man. A couple of blocks away, there's a huge Tasmanian devil."

Paige laughed. "I've always wondered if your folks named you after him."

"I sure hope not. But no telling what my parents were thinking back in those days."

Paige fell silent as Liane squealed from the window. Sometimes she struggled not to feel resentful when her best friends were having fun and all she could do was listen. Sometimes being blind was a total bummer and life seemed incredibly unfair.

Last night had been one of those times.

Now she raked her fingers through her short hair, wishing she could scrub the memories of last night out of her brain. She needed a positive outlook because today was an important day for YB2. The organizers of the Macy's Parade didn't invite just anybody to participate in their extravaganza, and YB2 had been given one of the best floats of all: the "Big Apple," the traditional float designed to honor New York City.

Aunt Rhonda, YB2's manager and publicist, had sent all the singers an e-mail explaining the float's significance. "It's a wonderful model of the city skyline," she had written. "It also features huge pieces of sports gear, so it's bound to please you guys. It's a huge thing—over thirty-seven feet long, with lots of room for all of you to sing and move around—carefully!—as you parade down Broadway. Taz will ride underneath the flatbed with the driver."

Paige and the others didn't need to be told that the New York City float would have special meaning this year. It had been years since the awful day of September 11, 2001, but no one had forgotten that more than three thousand people had died in that terrorist attack. New York City was still recovering from the disaster, and every member of YB2 wanted to honor the Big Apple.

They also wanted to perform for the fans across the country . . . if any of them made it out of bed in time to watch TV. Last night RC had reminded them that NBC's television cameras had been stationed at the viewing stand set up just before the end of the parade route. They'd stop there to sing their set, and approximately 60 million people would see that live television performance.

Paige had tried to imagine 60 million different people, all of them watching her, but her brain couldn't handle numbers that big.

She turned as she heard the bathroom door open. "It's all yours," Liane said, her voice muffled as if through a towel. "I'll dry my hair and do my makeup out here. What time are those girls from Macy's supposed to be here?"

Paige sighed as she stood and moved toward the bathroom. "Six-thirty, I think. I still don't understand why they're sending people to baby-sit us."

"They're not baby-sitting us, they're *escorting* us." The bed creaked as Liane sat on it. "RC said it's a great honor for them to be chosen as 'Macy's minders.'"

"Whatever." Shaking her head, Paige felt for the door frame, then stepped into the tiled bathroom. The floor felt cool under her bare feet, and the countertop wet under her fingertips. Liane had a habit of splashing water all over the place.

Paige reached for her velveteen toiletries case, then pulled out her toothbrush and toothpaste. She didn't really want a minder from Macy's or anywhere else. She'd spent fourteen years learning how to cope in a world where she couldn't see, and she didn't need some Macy's employee leading her through Central Park. The entire idea seemed like overkill, especially since Macy's had promised to send a minder for each member of YB2.

Muttering with every move, Paige brushed her teeth, washed her face, then swiped her underarms with deodorant. She pulled her overnight bag from beneath the vanity, then pulled fresh underwear from the silky "clean" bag. After taking off her pajamas, she stuffed them into the rough knit bag for dirty clothes.

She had a system for everything—packing her suitcase, reading her e-mail, putting on her makeup. She could apply lipstick without any help at all, and blush was fairly easy—as long as she had Liane check her cheeks afterward. Mascara could be tricky, so Paige settled for a light brush of her lashes with a smear of Vaseline. Since she wore dark glasses almost all the time, her eyes didn't usually show.

She lifted her overnight bag and moved back into the room. "Lee, check my face?"

A moment of silence, then Liane said, "Almost perfect. Wait a minute—"

Paige stood in silence as Liane rubbed at a spot on her cheek. "There. One side was darker than the other, but you're okay now."

"Thanks."

"Don't forget," Liane added, "it's going to be cold. We need to wear our wool socks and those undershirt things Aunt Rhonda sent us."

"Right," Paige said, even though the idea of having Aunt Rhonda dictate her clothing choices grated on her nerves. She loved her aunt—the woman had been like a mother to her ever since Paige's own mother had moved out when Paige was a baby—but sometimes Aunt Rhonda seemed to forget that Paige was a professional singer and almost independent.

Still . . . maybe she had a point about the cold. Paige had grown up in Florida, and when they traveled she was rarely out in the cold for more than a few minutes. Today they would spend all morning outside, and twenty-four degrees *was* below freezing.

She fumbled through her suitcase until she found the right items, then pulled them on. The tight thermal shirt warmed her almost instantly. If they didn't hurry and get outside, she was going to roast.

"I'm ready."

"Hang on. I can't get this thing over my head—"

Paige sank onto the bed as Liane struggled with her clothes, then stood when she heard the sound of a long zipper. She knew Liane was opening the costume bag that held their black outfits. Paige's costume consisted of black jeans, a black shirt, and a sheer silver-and-black skirt that swirled around her ankles when she swayed behind the piano. Liane, who moved around a lot more during the program, had been given black stretch jeans and a sequin-spattered top.

Paige had often tried to imagine what their costumes looked like, but she wasn't sure her mental image matched up with reality. Because her fingertips were her eyes, she could never know if what she imagined matched what everyone else saw.

She had just finished smoothing her skirt over her jeans when she heard a knock at the door. She touched the face of her Braille watch and read the time—6:25.

"If that's one of our escorts—" she moved toward the door—"they're early."

"It might be one of the guys," Liane called. "But check through the peephole before you open the door."

Paige sighed softly as she crossed to the door. She couldn't look through the peephole. Liane and the others were pretty good about catching themselves when they said stupid things like that, but occasionally they slipped up.

Paige pressed one hand to the door. "Who's there?"

"It's Melinda Grant," a young voice answered. "Your Macy's minder? I've come to escort Paige Clawson to the parade site."

Paige drew a deep breath. If not for this minor annoyance, it might be a perfect day.

2

Shane Clawson couldn't seem to pull himself away from the hotel room window. Behind him, Taz Trotter was checking his briefcase for spare batteries, wires, and connectors, but the only thing Shane had to bring to the parade was himself, a cell phone, and a sense of responsibility. Last night his dad had pulled him aside to remind him that he'd be directing the parade show because RC had to sit in the review stand with a group of TV producers.

"You can do it, Son," he'd said, crossing his arms as he smiled. "Just sing when you hear the music and wave when you don't. Make sure the others show up on time and don't trample all the flowers on the float. That's pretty much all there is to it."

Shane hadn't been exactly thrilled by his father's choice of words. What was the big deal about giving Shane

Paige

a job even a monkey could handle? If he had wanted to give Shane *real* responsibility, he'd have asked him to do something more complicated than making sure all the YB2 singers sang their best while they floated down Broadway.

The YB2 singers never gave less than their best. Hours of rehearsal and polished performances had turned them into singing, dancing robots. Sometimes Shane thought he would automatically sing and dance if he happened to hear one of their songs in his sleep.

But it wasn't all bad. Last night his dad had made a big deal about putting Shane in charge, telling all the singers and Taz that tomorrow they should give Shane all the respect they usually gave him. The others had nodded their agreement, but Shane had caught a couple of them looking at him with narrowed eyes. *Sure*, Noah's eyes seemed to be saying, *you're only in charge because you're the boss's son*.

And Liane, who could probably outthink and out-reason anybody on the team, had smiled while her eyes said, *Okay, big guy. We'll be watching, and we'll see how you do*.

Or maybe he was imagining things—maybe their eyes hadn't been saying anything at all. Maybe he was paranoid . . . and maybe he was a little scared that something would go wrong. After all, Taz was always talking about Murphy's Law—how if something could go wrong, you could bet that it would, and at the worst possible moment.

But what could go wrong on a beautiful day like today? He stood at the window and watched the sun rise over the city. A blanket of darkness still covered Central Park at this hour, but the streetlights buzzing the park shone bright, revealing crowds of people staking their positions on the sidewalks. According to the hotel concierge, the hundreds of parade participants began to line up at 5 a.m.; spectators began to arrive at six, complete with blankets, binoculars, and lawn chairs. They staked out their positions along Central Park West and Broadway, and for some people the chilly wait before the parade was as much fun as watching the parade itself.

"Paaaar-taaaaay," Shane murmured as envy pricked at him. He loved the Macy's parade; he had watched it every year as Aunt Rhonda baked the turkey and Dad made his predictions for the Bowl games. Before YB2, Shane would have given his right arm to have the opportunity to fly to New York, camp out on the street, and watch this parade. Now that he'd finally made it to the Big Apple, he had to be working *in* the parade, so he *still* couldn't watch it. But he'd asked Aunt Rhonda to tape it. When they were back in Orlando on break, maybe they could all get up early, make some cinnamon rolls, and sit around and watch it.

He leaned forward and pressed his hands against the window, feeling the sting of cold on his palms. "Man, that's frigid." He crossed his arms and shivered. "Gonna be wicked cold out there, Taz."

Taz snorted. "No kidding. But it could be worse. At least the sun'll be shining."

Shane turned from the window and took one last look

around the room. They'd been up since six, dressing quickly by lamplight. Shane had spent only five minutes on his hair this morning—a land speed record, by his estimation—but Taz had spent ten minutes fussing with the contents of his briefcase. If they didn't hurry, they'd be late, and nobody could be late today, especially not the guy in charge.

"Come on, it's fine." Shane tapped Taz's shiny silver briefcase as he walked by. "Man, you're like a grandma fussing with her purse. Relax. What could go wrong?"

Taz's jaw dropped. "You want me to tell you what could go wrong? A thousand things. If the wind picks up, we could get wind problems in those mikes. If you guys start moving around too much, you could mess up the placement of your mike or even lose it. And what about bleedover? I've got to be sure our wireless mikes don't conflict with the mikes on the float behind us and the one in front of us. And those parade people will have walkie-talkies and radios—I can't *wait* to see if those frequencies interfere with ours. A thousand things could go wrong today, and I just *know* I'll overlook something important—"

"Relax, man. You've never overlooked anything." Shane picked up a sock from the floor, then tossed it toward his open suitcase. "We'll be done with this gig by noon, then we can come back here and relax. In a few hours you'll forget any of this ever happened. I mean, it's not like NBC is going to let anything go wrong with the Macy's Thanksgiving Day Parade."

"Oh, yeah? You guys didn't think anything could go wrong at that place with the rolling floor, either."

Shane grinned as he moved into the bathroom to check his hair one last time. Taz had a point—they'd performed at a small gig last year, some rich kid's birthday party. The family had rented a hotel with a rolling stage that could be shoved back into the wall when they weren't using it. Without thinking, Taz and Shane had pulled out the stage and marked the front and back lines. The trouble began when the singers took their places on the front line, then rushed to the back line in a swift move—the stage rolled with them! Liane had nearly fallen on her rear, Paige and her piano had been slapped against the back wall, and Noah had fallen off the edge, landing right at some twelve-year-old girl's feet.

Not that she minded much.

Shane squinted into the mirror, gave his hair a final shot of spray, then reached into the closet for his black leather jacket. They might freeze until the parade began, but they would warm up once they started performing—nothing like a little movement to get the blood circulating. And though they were only doing two songs, they would sing that two-song set as long as it took the parade to navigate from Seventy-seventh Street to Thirty-fourth.

Shane heard a knock on the door. Peering through the peephole, he saw two attractive young women in navy blazers and dark slacks—the minders from Macy's.

"Hey, Taz," he called over his shoulder. "We got girls out here. You ready?"

Sighing, Taz snapped his briefcase, then stood and took another look around the room. "I guess."

"Then let's go."

Shane opened the door, then gave the two visitors a smile the size of Texas. "Good morning, ladies. Are you ready for us?"

The first girl, dark haired and about eighteen, lifted a brow. "We're ready if you are."

"We're ready for anything." With a spring in his step, Shane put out his arm, felt the brunette slip her arm through his, and led the way to the elevator.

Macy's. You gotta hand it to them, those people thought of *everything*.

3

"So, Melinda." Stepping into the hall with her cane in her hand, Paige tried to be pleasant. "Have you worked for Macy's very long?"

"Six months." The girl took a sudden quick breath. "Um . . . would you like to hold my hand or something? They told me you were blind, so I know I need to be extra careful with you."

Paige bit back an exasperated sigh. When her escort had introduced herself, Paige had nearly told Melinda Grant to take the morning off; Paige could easily walk with Liane and her minder, but Melinda had sounded so excited, even awed.

Now Liane and her minder had moved out of earshot, leaving Paige in the hall with an overactive do-gooder who smelled of flowers—strong, superfragrant ones, in fact. Either she used cheap perfume, or she'd bathed in a gallon of roses this morning.

"You don't have to hold my hand." Paige lifted her cane. "I'll walk beside you and use this. You can tell me, though, when we reach the elevator or steps."

"Oh. Okay." The girl began to walk with slow steps. Paige followed, matching her strides to the sound of Melinda's heavy shoes on the carpet.

"How old are you?" Paige asked, not knowing what else to say. Good grief, in a minute she'd be asking where Melinda went to school and what she wanted to be when she got out of college . . . stupid questions, really, but they always seemed to get the conversation rolling with starstruck fans who didn't know what to say.

"I'm sixteen."

"Umm. I'm fourteen. So you're older than me."

"Wow. That's incredible."

"Not really. You were born first."

"But you seem so much older."

"Well . . . I've been on the road awhile. That can make you grow up pretty fast."

"Yeah, I guess so. I know I've grown up a lot since I started dating my boyfriend. He's older, too."

"Really?" Despite her annoyance with the situation, Paige felt a stirring of curiosity. "How old is he?"

"Nineteen. Since I've been hanging out with him and his friends, I feel a lot older. My mom says she's noticed a big change in me—though she's not sure she likes it."

Paige digested this news in silence. She'd never had a boyfriend. With YB2's hectic concert schedule, she wasn't likely to have one any time soon.

"Here's the elevator."

Paige halted, then heard a plastic clicking sound as Melinda's nails tapped the button.

Uncomfortable in the silence, Paige laced her fingers together around her cane. "Um . . . so what's the plan for this morning?"

Melinda's tone brightened. "Oh, that's easy. First I take you downstairs where we have our picture taken for the Macy's employee bulletin board. Then I have to escort you to the greenroom, where they have coffee and doughnuts and juice if you want something to eat. They'll even cook you breakfast if you want. You can take your time and eat. After that, whenever you're ready, I'll walk you into Central Park and we'll find your float—it's the Big Apple, right?"

Paige nodded. "That's what they tell me."

"The Big Apple is number fifteen in the lineup. After we get there, I'm supposed to ask you if there's anything else you need. If there isn't, I leave you there and hurry back here for debriefing."

Paige forced a smile. "Sounds like a very official mission."

"Oh, it is. You wouldn't believe how many clerks wanted to be celebrity minders. To get this job we had to have a perfect attendance record at the store, plus we had to write an essay on why we thought we deserved the honor. And we couldn't have a single customer complaint on our record, not one."

"Wow . . . and what department do you work in?"

Melinda giggled. "You won't believe it. I sell these teeny tiny designer baby shoes. It's hilarious. I don't even have to try them on or anything; the moms just come in to buy them. I think I've got the best job in the entire store. It's not my dream career, not something I want to do forever, but it's pretty good for now. Of course *you* have a dream job, traveling all around the country, meeting famous people, getting to do cool things like this—"

Paige forced another smile. "It is pretty cool."

The elevator opened with a tinny *ding*. Paige waited as the doors slid open. "Is it full?"

"Oh, no, it's empty," Melinda said, stepping forward. "Come on in. It'll take us right down to the lower lobby where the photographer is waiting."

Still smiling, Paige stepped into the elevator, then turned to face the doors. She would probably keep this stiff smile on her face all morning . . . at least until she reached the float and could relax.

4

Twenty minutes later, Paige's patience had vanished. Bad enough that Melinda dragged her to a place where a photographer took at least four pictures of Paige smiling and Melinda doing only who knew what, but then the girl led Paige to a table, made her sit, then crammed a sticky glazed doughnut into her hand. Paige tried to explain that she didn't like to eat sweets so early in the morning, but then Melinda went off in search of a hot breakfast for her celebrity, leaving Paige afraid to move lest she drop the doughnut on a clean table or smear some passerby's coat with the sugary mess.

Only when Paige felt the round edge of a plate on the table did she feel safe in dropping the messy doughnut. "Melinda?" she asked, hoping to find a napkin. "Are you there?"

For someone who'd practically taken a vow not to

leave Paige's side, the girl was awfully hard to find. Paige turned her head, listening for Melinda's voice, and finally heard her.

"See her down there? That's my girl. Paige, you know, from YB2. Oh, yeah, I'd hoped to escort one of the guys, but Sean wouldn't have liked that." She giggled, a high-pitched sound that carried even better than her voice.

Paige exhaled slowly, then groped around the table-top for a napkin someone might have dropped. No luck, but she did almost spill a cup of coffee.

Down at the end of the table, Melinda seemed determined to exhibit Paige like some kind of trained monkey. "Look who I've got," she called to someone else. "Paige Clawson, the blind girl from YB2. She's cute, huh? You should see her get around. She's really good. You wouldn't know she was blind if . . . well, if you didn't know."

Paige felt like a captured animal. While she sat there, quietly feeling nauseous from the scents of bacon, scrambled eggs, and greasy hash browns, Melinda kept calling and laughing and probably pointing. Paige didn't need eyes to know what was happening at the end of the table. To make matters worse, though she strained her ears, she couldn't hear any of her friends' voices.

Finally, when her patience had worn completely thin, Paige raised her voice enough to cut through Melinda's babble. "Please!" she shouted, "Can I say something?"

The sharp tone in her voice must have caught Melinda's attention. Immediately the girl fell silent.

"What time do I have to be at the float?" Paige asked.

Melinda's footsteps hurried closer. "Um . . . eight o'clock, I think. They want everyone in position by eight so they can pull around and line up all the floats."

"And what time is it now?"

"About fifteen minutes after seven."

"And how long will it take us to find the float in the park?"

"Um . . . maybe twenty minutes. Not too long."

Paige nodded. "Okay. So I have some time to get cleaned up. Can you please point me toward a ladies' room? I need to get all this sugar off my hand."

"Oh. Sorry." Melinda must have finally noticed the mess on Paige's palm because she began to swipe at the stickiness with a napkin. "I can get it off—"

"Thanks, but I'd really like to use a ladies' room. I need soap and water."

"Oh. Okay."

"And would you mind taking my plate away, please? I just can't eat a hot breakfast this early in the morning."

"Oh." Melinda lifted the plate from the table. "Anything else?"

"Thanks, but that's great. If you can lead me toward the restroom, I'd really appreciate it."

"Come with me, then. There's one right around the corner. Just let me dump this plate, then we'll go."

Paige stiffened as Melinda grabbed her elbow and began to tug her forward. The room was buzzing with people now, a crowd of men and women—people from

Macy's, certainly, and at least a few celebrities who were also scheduled to appear in the parade.

Were they all having as much fun as she was?

After hearing the muffled *whoosh* of her breakfast scoring a basket in the nearest garbage can, Paige followed Melinda into a carpeted hallway. They walked forward a few more steps, then paused. Paige heard a door squeak.

"This is the ladies' room," Melinda said. "Do you want me to come in with you?"

"No, thanks, I can handle this myself. By the way, Melinda—did you see any of the other YB2 singers in the room?"

"Um . . . yeah. The other girl was standing over by the doughnuts, and Noah was talking to some people by the juice machine."

So the others *were* around. And if Paige could ditch Melinda and hook up with Liane or Noah, she'd be out of her misery.

She gave Melinda what she hoped was a charming smile. "You know what? Orange juice sounds really good right now. Could you get me a cup? I don't drink coffee, but I sure like juice!"

"Okay." A note of doubt filled Melinda's voice. "Are you sure you're gonna be okay in there? I'm not supposed to let you out of my sight for a minute."

"Well . . . didn't you leave me at breakfast?"

"Not really—I kept my eye on you the entire time."

Paige forced a laugh. "You don't have to keep an eye

on me in the bathroom, Melinda. Where am I going to go?"

"Okay, then."

Paige stepped inside the bathroom and let the outer door close, then felt a second door and opened it. She had to hurry.

Moving as quickly as she dared, she went into the bathroom, found the sink by tapping the wall with her cane, then washed the sticky mess from her hands. She slapped her hands against her skirt rather than run the noisy hand dryer—a little dampness on her clothes wouldn't matter, but she'd jump out of her skin if Melinda crept up behind her while the hand dryer was roaring.

Paige pressed her shoulder against the inner door, then pushed the first door open and waited, her ears scanning the corridor for any sounds of movement. Nothing.

Moving as quickly as she dared, she began walking back the way they had come. She was taking a tremendous risk by leaving, but if she ran into Melinda she could always say she had grown tired of waiting and set out to look for the girl. If she was lucky, though, she would slip through the crowd, find one of the other YB2 members, and step outside without ever seeing Melinda again.

Hearing the dull roar of conversation, Paige lifted her head and listened for familiar voices. She heard the squeak and slap of an opening door and walked toward it, then felt the sun and cold air on her face.

Whoa—had she gone *outside*? She had never dreamed

the breakfast room was next to an outdoor exit, but that made sense—from here, the escorts were supposed to walk their people to Central Park. So she was probably standing on a sidewalk next to the hotel, with Central Park on the other side of the street.

"Hey, I know you! You're Paige Clawson, right? My daughter loves your music!"

Paige blinked at the unfamiliar female voice. "Um . . . hi."

The stranger kept talking. "I can't believe it's really you. Can I have your autograph?"

Smiling, Paige held up her hand. "Sorry. I'm on a schedule this morning, and I seem to have lost my escort. If you'll excuse me—"

"Sure, and isn't that always the way it is? A kid no older than my own daughter tells me she's too busy to sign her name on a slip of paper. Fine. See if I ever buy your music again."

Paige felt a blush burn her cheeks as her father's words came rolling back on a wave of memory. He was always stressing that what they did *off* the platform was more important than what they did *on* it, and signing autographs was such a small thing.

"I'd sign," Paige struggled to explain, "but I don't have any paper or a pen."

"I've got that," and sure enough, a moment later a slip of paper and a pen landed in Paige's bare palm. Pasting a smile on her face, she leaned on the glass door behind her and scratched out her name.

"Here you go." She held out the paper, only to find it snatched away and *another* sheet between her fingers.

"Oh, me too! Can you make it to Tiffany? Put 'To my best friend, Tiff, from Paige Clawson.'"

Paige turned and began to scrawl on the paper. She had no idea if her writing was even legible, but at the moment she didn't care what the final result looked like.

"For Tiffany," she said. She turned and offered the sheet to whomever had handed it to her, then found her hands filled with two, no, three more papers.

Good grief, how had all these fans found their way onto this street? She'd never get to Central Park if one of the other YB2 singers didn't come along to rescue her.

She signed frantically as voices rose from the mob around her.

"Hey, who is that?"

"It's the girl from YB2."

"Liane?"

"No, the other one. The one with the glasses."

"Paige Clawson? She's here on the street?"

Signing as quickly as her rapidly freezing fingers would allow, Paige scribbled her name on slips of paper and tossed them over her shoulder as a mass of humanity pressed closer and closer.

5

Walking through the park with Miss Jocelyn David, a girl pretty enough to be a model, Shane spied several of his teammates along the winding park paths. Noah was gesturing wildly as he gabbed with his escort, a petite girl with long red hair, and Josiah was walking silently beside his Macy's minder, a tall guy with pimples, slicked back hair, and glasses. Shane spied Liane and her escort a few steps behind Josiah, and behind them walked Billy Joel and his silver-haired Macy's minder—a woman who couldn't be a day under sixty.

Shane grinned. He loved this gig already, and they hadn't even sung a note.

"Here's your float." Jocelyn pointed to the huge float parked by the curb. "It's nice, isn't it?"

"Wow—it's cool," Shane agreed. He let out a long, low

Paige

whistle as they walked around the incredible creation. The buildings and sports symbols on the float had been made entirely of small plastic strips stuffed into wire netting. Someone had spent *hours* forming these incredible shapes.

He and Jocelyn walked the entire length of both sides, then she paused by a stepladder someone had placed at the edge.

"It was a pleasure to escort you," she said, lowering her gaze as she blushed.

"The pleasure was mine," Shane answered. He wanted to say something else, maybe even ask this girl out to a movie or something, but the group had a dinner to go to tonight. Maybe . . . then again, maybe not.

Life on the road was harder than most people realized.

"You've been great," Shane said, placing his foot on the bottom rung of the ladder. As an afterthought, he leaned forward and gave Jocelyn a quick kiss on the cheek. "Thanks so much."

She brought her hand to her cheek and smiled, then she turned and moved away with a quick step. Shane watched her go, then turned and climbed the stepladder.

The designers had built a curving pathway over the long surface of the float that reminded Shane of the yellow brick road from *The Wizard of Oz*. Five small circles had been scattered across the surface, each one in front of some symbol of New York athletics—a giant baseball, a bat, a football, a hockey puck, and a basketball. These had been crafted with incredible attention to detail. The baseball even had red stitching.

"That's where you stand—right in front of the baseball."

Shane looked up as a man's voice reached his ear—the fellow on the ground caught Shane's eye, then reached up for a handshake. "Hi. I'm Bob Stiller, a production manager from Macy's. We're glad to have you kids with us. I understand you'll be running things today."

"Yes, that's right. I'm Shane." Shane felt heat burn the back of his neck as he released the man's hand and straightened. Apparently Mr. Stiller didn't think it was odd to place a sixteen-year-old in charge of the most important float in the parade.

"Good to meet you, Shane. So—what do you think?"

Slipping his hands into his pockets, Shane looked at the "Big Apple" and whistled again. "It's incredible, Mr. Stiller. This float and the entire parade. I've watched it on television for years, but I had no idea things were this complicated."

"You can call me Bob." The man laughed as he propped one foot on the stepladder. "You wouldn't believe what an undertaking this is. Thousands of people are involved every year, and the manpower—well, it's impossible to measure all of it. But we have great volunteers, and Macy's has always been generous in its support. Ever since 1924, when those first few immigrants employed at Macy's decided to throw a parade, this event goes on as scheduled, rain, sleet, or snow. Nothing stops the Macy's Thanksgiving Parade."

Shane rested his hands on his hips and shivered as a gust of cold wind lifted his hair. "Let's hope it doesn't snow today."

"It won't." Bob grinned. "Nothing but sunny skies today; I checked the weather report first thing this morning. Now, let me show you where your singers will be standing."

With surprising agility, Bob climbed the stepladder and hopped onto the float. "These circles are for your performers," he said, pointing to the wooden areas on the platform. "And these metal stands are for you to grip or lean against if the wind picks up. You probably won't need 'em, but the wind can be fierce when it comes barreling between those tall buildings. We can get a real wind tunnel effect that's nothing to laugh at."

Shane nodded. "We'll be careful."

"This—" Bob walked over to another area, then lifted a disguised trapdoor—"is the entrance to the cab. This is where I'll be driving and your sound engineer will be working to keep you guys sounding good. You'll see there are monitors in the floor—" he pointed to several mesh screens that had been cleverly hidden among the decorations—"and speakers within the design structures. Trust me, the sound is good. We tested it last night."

"I trust you—but I know Taz will want to do a sound check as soon as he arrives." Shane gazed down into the cab. "Pretty cozy down there, huh?"

Bob laughed. "That's a good word for it. We aren't able to see much except the road straight ahead, but I'll have a radio to communicate with the parade officials. We'll keep a slow and steady pace until we hit the viewing stands—the first one's at Columbus Circle and the second's at Thirty-fourth Street. You'll perform your set at each location, but the last one is where you'll be playing to the TV cameras." He grinned. "NBC will want you to be looking good by the time you get there."

Shane nodded. "Got it. We ran through all this last night."

"Good. Okay—" Bob rubbed his gloved hands together and looked around—"we want everybody aboard by eight, and then we pull around and line up to wait for the countdown. Are most of your people here?"

Shane turned to study the area. Several booths were set up in the park. Taz and Liane were picking up cups of hot cocoa from one, while a few feet away Josiah and Noah were munching on breakfast burritos—eating *again*—and talking with their escorts.

For an instant, he wished he weren't in charge. If he didn't have to be up here with Mr. Stiller, he could be down there with Jocelyn David, sipping hot coffee and looking into her brown eyes. She had the nicest smile . . .

He shrugged away the thought. Responsibility had its price.

He glanced at his watch. "We're only missing one," he said. "My sister. But it's early yet, so maybe she stopped for something."

Bob nodded, then turned as if to study the line of pedestrians moving outside the gate around Central Park. A pair of security guards at the gate were checking ID badges as people entered.

"Do you think she had problems with her ID?"

"No—she had to be with a Macy's escort. Maybe they got held up back in the hotel." He forced a smile as he met Bob's gaze. "You know how girls are. Knowing Paige, she spilled something on her outfit and had to spend thirty minutes in the bathroom trying to clean up."

The words had sprung easily to his lips, but Paige really wasn't the type to be distracted by spills or other accidents. And she wasn't usually late. But today she was with someone else, so maybe that person had a problem with tardiness.

Bob pulled a radio from his belt. "Should I call security?"

Shane looked at his watch again. Seven-fifty-five, so Paige wasn't technically late. She and her escort might have stopped for a snack along the way, or maybe they were simply taking their time.

"Let's give her five more minutes," he said, crossing his arms. "I'm sure she'll show up."

6

"I'm sorry, but I have to go." Flattened against the glass door, Paige held her hands up in a don't-shoot pose. "I can't sign anything else; I'm late."

"Just one more?"

"But I'm your biggest fan!"

"Come on, one more!"

"I'm sorry, but I can't." She tried to smile, but the best she could manage was a grimace. Tears danced behind her eyes. In a minute she was going to experience meltdown in front of all these people; she was going to scream and claw and fight her way through them or drop to the side-walk in a panicked fit.

"There you are! Hey! Move it! I need that girl!"

Paige looked up, sheer relief swallowing her fear as she recognized the voice. "Melinda?"

"It's me, Paige. How in the world did you get out here?"

"I . . . took a wrong turn, I guess."

"Good grief, girl, you're standing on the sidewalk where everybody can see you. Let me get you back inside."

Abandoning her pride, Paige gave Melinda her hand. The girl dragged Paige forward, ignoring the calls and comments as she opened the glass door and led Paige back into the quiet hallway next to the breakfast room . . . which no longer buzzed with any kind of activity at all.

Alarm bells rang in Paige's head. "Where is everybody?"

"Where we should be—on the floats, probably. Come on, I have to take you out through the protected exit. There's a protected walkway with a line of security guards to make sure no one busts through, and they're checking IDs at all the park entrances."

"What time is it?"

Melinda halted. "Stink. It's 7:59. There's no way we're going to make it to your float in time."

"But the parade doesn't start until nine."

"They move the floats at eight. They're scattered all over the place right now, but as soon as everyone's aboard, they line 'em up around the block."

Paige bit her lip as Melinda breathed heavily. "Okay, we're not going to panic. We're going to have to forget the park and find your float in the lineup. I have my badge, so I can get us past the security guards at the starting point, but we'll have to walk awhile to get to them."

Paige didn't like the sound of Plan B. "How far will we have to walk?"

"Well . . . your float is number fifteen, right? That's good, fifteen spaces can't be more than four or five blocks once we reach the point where they start lining everybody up. The starting position is probably six or seven blocks away."

Paige closed her eyes as a feeling of helplessness swept over her. Boy oh boy, she'd blown it this time. She hadn't done something little like forget a line or miss a cue. Oh, no. She'd waited until the biggest gig of the year, then she had committed the unthinkable sin—she had missed a call time.

Shane would be fuming.

Her dad was going to kill her—or at least ground her for life.

She pressed her hand to her forehead, trying to think of a way out of this mess. Melinda didn't exactly inspire confidence, and Paige wasn't sure they could walk six or seven blocks through a mob like the one outside.

"How can we move through the crowd?" she asked, hating the whimper in her voice. "You saw what happened out on the sidewalk. If I go out and someone recognizes me, we'll be stopped—we might be trapped. We'll never make it to the float in time if we are."

"Wait, let me think." Melinda fell silent, but her shoe tapped the floor, sending a staccato beat through Paige's brain. "Okay! I've got it. My boyfriend's van is parked only a couple of blocks from here—it's not far, and it's away from the parade route, so there won't be as many people. I'll take you to the van and we'll get him to drive us up to the starting point."

"But . . . aren't the roads blocked off?"

"Only right around Central Park. He can drive us north and west, so we'll only have to walk a couple of blocks east instead of ten blocks north through the crowds. Okay?"

"But we've still got to walk to the van. How are we supposed to get to it without anybody stopping us?"

"Easy. Here."

Melinda pressed something over Paige's head. She flinched, then gingerly fingered the soft object.

"A hat?"

"It's big, so no one will see your brown hair. You're already wearing glasses, so that'll help, and that black jacket blends right in. So just grab my hand and I'll lead you to the van. I know right where to find Sean—he parked in an alley out back and I was supposed to meet him there after I dropped you off. We were going to listen to the parade on the radio."

"Well . . . okay."

With no other choice, Paige held out her hand and let Melinda lead her away.

7

Shane reached down to help Liane from the ladder to the float, then directed her toward the circle in front of the giant hockey puck. Josiah and Noah had already climbed aboard and found their positions by the basketball and football, and Taz had disappeared into the cab beneath the deck. Only one space remained open, the circle in front of the ten-foot baseball bat. Taz had made certain that Paige's keyboard made it to the float, but there was no sign of the girl who should be standing behind it.

Noah must have caught Shane's worried expression. "Good grief, dude, you don't think she's lost, do you?"

"How could she be lost?" Shane tried to keep his voice calm, but his palms were damp. How could she do this to him today? She knew RC had left him in charge, so maybe she was taking advantage. Maybe she was late on purpose, a little sisterly payback for all the times he'd made her life crazy.

He turned to Liane. "She was with her escort when you last saw her, right?"

She nodded. "She left the room the same time I did. And I saw her getting her picture taken outside the greenroom, so I know she made it that far."

"I saw her with a doughnut," Noah added. "She didn't look very thrilled with it."

"So—what could have happened?"

"Shane?"

He turned to the trapdoor, where Bob Stiller's head had appeared in the opening. "It's 8:00. We need to pull around and get into position."

Shane swallowed hard. "My sister's not here yet."

"Maybe she'll catch up." Bob's eyes crinkled as his mouth curved in an expression that could hardly be called a smile. "Listen, I'll put a call out on the radio, okay? We'll have all the guards looking for her, and we'll have them tell her to meet us in the lineup. Can you tell me what she looks like?"

"She has brown hair," Shane answered. "About five four, average build, wearing black jeans, a skirt, and a black leather jacket. Short hair. And she always wears black glasses because she's blind."

"Oh, man. I'll get right on it." Bob disappeared into the cab and a moment later Shane heard the squawk and hiss of a radio.

He looked up at the sky, where the morning sun was

jabbing bright spears of light through the skeletal dark trees of the park. In a minute, he'd have to call his dad and tell him they'd hit a problem . . . a big one. And RC would groan and mutter something about responsibility, and Shane would feel like a complete failure on the most important day of his career.

Paige, where are you?

His eyes scanned the rolling pathways and the people walking by, but he saw no one who looked like his sister.

He flinched when the huge float shuddered to life beneath their feet. Liane moved to her position and rested her arms on the metal support bar. Noah took his place beside the football, but by his crossed arms and faintly accusing expression Shane knew Noah wasn't impressed with his leadership.

He glanced from Noah to Josiah. "Did either of you guys see Paige on your way here?"

Both guys shook their heads.

"Okay, then." With heavy fingers, Shane pulled his phone from his pocket, flipped it open, and punched in the number to his father's cell phone.

8

Shivering in the icy wind, Paige ducked her head and followed Melinda with heavy steps that slapped the pavement. She had tried using her cane, but Melinda was walking too quickly and the crowds were too thick. Though she couldn't see where they were going, she could sense the press of people and knew they were moving against the tide. Everyone else wanted to walk west, toward the park, while she and Melinda were heading east.

At last Melinda spoke. "Finally! There's the van."

Paige sighed in relief when Melinda dropped her hand and left her on the sidewalk. They had managed to keep a brisk pace despite the crowd, and Paige's tense nerves had made her heart beat faster.

She touched the face of her Braille watch as Melinda spoke with someone a few feet away. Eight-ten, so she

Paige

was already late. Thank goodness Melinda had come up with an alternate idea, or they might have missed the parade altogether.

She could hear the girl talking to someone, then a male voice answered. Not wanting to intrude, Paige reached for her cane she'd tucked under her arm . . . and realized it was missing.

She bit back a scream of frustration. She'd been wearing so many clothes she hadn't felt it slip away as they hurried through the crowd. She'd never find it now, and there wasn't time to look.

"Hey there," Melinda said, coming toward her, then leading her forward. "Sean says it's okay, he'll drive us up to the parade starting point. Now watch the curb. You'll need to step down. The van only has two seats, so you and I are going to ride in the back."

A van with only two seats? Paige's mental image of a roomy passenger vehicle vanished, especially when the back door opened with a rusty creak.

"Here." Melinda tugged on her elbow. "Lean forward and kinda crawl in. We can sit on the floor."

Paige put out her hand and immediately felt the slickness of grease. The air in the van was heavy, filled with the scents of oil and cigarettes and something else . . . maybe beer?

She crinkled her nose. "Um . . . I'm wearing performance clothes, Melinda. Do you have anything I could sit on?"

Melinda hesitated, then called, "Brian? Can you shove

that old blanket this way? I need to spread it out on the floor."

Some other voice grunted, then Paige heard a soft thud, followed by several bumps and thumps. A moment later, Melinda called from inside the van. "Okay, I've got it spread out. So climb on in, and we'll run you up to Seventy-seventh Street. After that, we'll only have to walk a couple of blocks before we find the start of the parade."

"Hey, Mel," a male voice called from the driver's seat, "we should probably go up to Eighty-sixth. I mean, if her float is pretty far along in the parade, they'll be lined up farther north."

"Yeah." Melinda took Paige's arm and guided her into a sitting position on the ridged floor. "Sean's right. We should probably go farther up, then cut over. That sounds right."

"But you said there were security guards at the entrance." Paige crossed her legs. "If we miss the entrance, how are we supposed to get through?"

"You duck under the barricades—we do it all the time." Another guy spoke from the front passenger seat, and Paige guessed that Melinda hadn't thought to introduce either guy.

"Whatever," Paige answered. "I just need to get there fast. And I need to call my brother—do any of you have a cell phone?"

For an instant no one answered, then Melinda said, "Sean? Don't you have your phone with you?"

"Yeah."

A moment later Melinda placed a phone in Paige's hand. Paige ran her fingertip over the keyboard, then shook her head and handed it back. "I'm not familiar with that kind. Will you dial the number for me? It's 407-555-3847."

She listened to the phone's tiny *beep beep* as Melinda punched in the number, then sighed when she felt the phone in her hand again. She held it to her ear, her heart pounding, then closed her eyes when the call connected . . . with a taped "all circuits are busy" message.

She lowered the phone. Thanksgiving was probably a busy time for callers, probably right up there with Christmas and Mother's Day. Telephone service could be iffy all day long.

She'd have to wait.

9

RC answered on the first ring. "Hello?"

Shane swallowed the lump of frustration in his throat. "Dad, it's me. We've got a little problem here . . . Paige never showed up at the float. We're pulling around to line up, and Bob, our driver, has told all the security guards to keep an eye out for her. But . . . well, I thought you ought to know what's happening."

Shane had never known his father to be at a loss for words, but silence followed his announcement.

Finally, his father's voice croaked over the line. "You say they've alerted security?"

"Yes."

"And she left the hotel room with her Macy's escort?"

"Yeah, Lee saw them leave together."

RC muttered something under his breath, but Shane couldn't make out the words.

Paige

"Dad?"

"Man, I wish Paige and Lee had stayed together."

"I know."

He could almost hear his father's thoughts racing. "Okay, keep on that Bob guy and make sure he updates security. Keep your phone in your pocket; Paige will probably try to call you. It isn't like her to not show up."

"I know."

"You've got nearly an hour before the parade begins. Just do what you have to do and let's hope someone finds Paige before the parade starts to roll. Tell Taz he might have to run the piano track if Paige doesn't get aboard in time."

Shane's gaze shifted to the keyboard, which had been sturdily mounted to the float. Paige was supposed to stand behind it and play as well as sing, but in a moment of foresight they had recorded her piano part on a backup track.

"I'm sure she'll show up, Dad. Maybe her escort got turned around or something."

"I'm sure you're right, Son. Keep me informed, okay? I'll see if I can light a fire under some security people at this end."

Shane hung up the phone, then dropped it back into his pocket. Paige didn't have a cell phone with her—at the moment, Shane was carrying the group's emergency phone and RC had his personal phone—but she was bright enough to ask for help if she needed it. Surely she'd call if she could.

Telling himself there was absolutely no reason to panic, Shane gripped the metal stand behind his back as the float shuddered and rolled forward.

10

Paige shifted uneasily as the van moved forward, then stopped in the street, the muffler rumbling noisily beyond the closed double doors. She could smell exhaust among the other odors in the vehicle, and the foul stink did nothing to set her mind at ease.

"Why'd we stop?" She turned to the front, where the two guys had been talking in low tones beneath a blaring radio.

"Gridlock," Brian called from the passenger's seat. "So many roads are blocked off for the parade, you know, so the traffic that can move is moving real slow."

"I, uh, hate to be a pain," she pushed herself up to her knees, "but I really need to reach the float. Do you see a police officer anywhere? Maybe if we flagged one down, he could find a way to get me to the parade."

From behind the wheel, Melinda's boyfriend chuckled.

The edge in his laughter sent a flicker of worry coursing through her limbs.

"What a princess," he said, scorn lining his voice. The seat creaked and Paige sank to the floor, sensing that he had turned to look at her. "You think you're so special this traffic's going to split for you like Charlton Heston and the Blue Sea?"

Paige lifted her chin. "You mean Moses and the Red Sea," she answered quietly. "Heston was the actor playing Moses."

Sean snorted. "Whatever. Just sit back and stay quiet, Your Highness. We'll get you there when we get you there."

Paige turned to Melinda, then lowered her voice. "Will you call my brother again?"

"I don't think so." Paige felt a shiver climb her spine when Sean answered. "What good would it do?"

"Well, it'd stop him from worrying," Paige went on, cautiously feeling her way through the conversation. "He can be a pain sometimes, but he really does worry about me."

"All right, I'll call," Sean said, "if you'll sit back and relax. The number's still in the phone."

Paige sank back, but though she strained her ears for the tiny *beep beep* sounds of the phone, she heard nothing but the static of the radio as Brian searched for a station.

After a moment, she heard the phone click shut.

"Nobody home," Sean said. "He doesn't pick up."

She shook her head. "You must have—might have—misdialed. Shane would pick up no matter what. He's bound to be worried about—"

"I told you, he didn't answer. I know I'm right because unlike *some* people, I don't make stupid mistakes."

Was that anger directed at her . . . or at Melinda? Paige wanted to scream in frustration, but instead she turned toward the back and wished she had paid more attention to the last few vans the group had rented. She had no idea how van doors opened, where the handle was, or if the doors were locked. If she raised herself up to fumble with the mechanism, the guys up front would be sure to see her movements.

So what if they did? She could probably get help faster on the street than sitting here in the back of this stinky van.

She had risen to her knees when the van lunged forward then swerved sharply as Sean changed lanes. Paige fell back, lost her balance, and hit her head on something hard.

"Oh my goodness!" Melinda yelled, pawing at Paige's head and shoulders. "Are you okay?"

Grimacing, Paige pressed one hand to the back of her head, then pulled it away and ran her thumb over a warm stickiness on her fingers.

"Ow," she said, her heart pounding, "I think I'm bleeding."

11

"You're kidding." Doubt gleamed in Noah's eyes. "We're performing without Paige?"

Shane lifted his hands in helplessness. "What else are we supposed to do? She's not here."

"We should call security!"

"We've done that."

"Then we should call the police."

Shane shrugged. "We don't know if a crime has been committed, Noah. She's lost. The security people have her description and they're looking for her. And she's with her Macy's escort."

Liane's eyes had gone round. "What if the escort . . . is some kind of *terrorist*?"

Shane forced a laugh. "Come on, Lee, get real. You said her escort was a girl."

"Well . . . girls can be terrorists, too."

"I doubt Macy's would let a terrorist escort a celebrity to their parade. No, Paige and her escort got lost in the crowd, but they'll find their way to the float eventually. In the meantime we have a job to do. Because we are professionals, we're going to do it."

Liane crossed her arms. "Good grief, you sound just like RC."

Shane waited to see if the others had any smart remarks, but Josiah turned and moved to his position; after a moment, Noah did the same thing. Only Liane lingered, a look of accusation in her eyes.

What did she expect him to do? He wasn't a cop, and this wasn't a movie. It was a Thanksgiving parade, and Paige had wandered off and gotten herself lost, that's all. No big hairy deal. Come to think of it, he wouldn't have been surprised to learn that Paige had wandered off on purpose. She hated needing special attention and she rarely asked for it. And she hadn't been thrilled by the idea of the Macy's minders.

Ignoring Liane's hot glare, Shane leaned against the metal brace at his position and crossed his arms. But as the float edged slowly over the road, passing vendors and security guards and volunteers in bright red vests, he found himself searching for his sister's head among a sea of strangers.

12

Battling fear and increasing tension, Paige sat
in the back of the van with a smelly rag pressed to the
cut on the back of her head. Melinda had assured Paige
the cut wasn't bad, and the bleeding did seem to have
stopped. But her head was killing her, and the two clowns
in the front seat seemed not to care that their crazy driving had nearly knocked Paige out cold.

They'd been zigzagging through the streets of Manhattan for the last half hour. Twice Paige had been ready
to edge toward the back and search for a way out of the
van, but each time a reassuring cry from Melinda had
stopped her. "Seventy-first Street! We're making good
time now, Paige! Just hang on and we'll get you there!"

Paige had asked Sean to call Shane again, and again
Sean said he was calling but she didn't hear a sound from
the phone. Finally she put out her hand and forced her

voice to sound relaxed: "I hate to keep bothering you, Sean, so why don't you let me dial? I'll figure out the numbers."

"It's no trouble," he had insisted. "I'm telling you, he's not answering his phone."

"Want me to try?" Brian asked.

"Relax, man, I'll try again in a minute."

Paige was crouching in the back, her chin propped on her knees, when she heard a steady *clomp clomp clomp* from outside the van. For an instant she wondered at the odd sound, then her brain placed it—horse's hooves! Policemen in New York rode horses, especially in parades!

"Hey!" She leaned toward the front of the van, "that's a cop outside, right? Stop him! Ask him if he'll take me to the parade route."

"That's no cop, it's a tourist buggy," Brian answered.

Sean gunned the engine in response, and after a minute Paige could no longer hear the sound of hooves. "We're making progress," Sean said as the van settled back into stillness. "There was a break in the traffic."

"But we're not moving *now*," Paige pointed out.

"Hey," Brian said, "are you *really* that girl from YB2?"

She dropped her head to her knees. "Yeah."

"Boy, it must be nice to be you. You get to travel and meet people and make all kinds of money."

"The money goes into a trust fund," Paige answered, "and it's not going to be much fun to be me when I catch up with the others. I'm going to be in *so* much trouble."

"Oh, I feel *awful*," Melinda wailed. "I can't believe I lost you. This is all my fault."

Paige said nothing. At the moment she wanted nothing more than to blame Melinda for this entire mess, but it wasn't the other girl's fault, not really. Paige had gotten herself into this situation by trying to give Melinda the slip. If she had stayed with her escort the way she was supposed to, Paige would probably be standing at her keyboard right now.

"Maybe you won't be in trouble," Brian called from the front. "Maybe you can convince them it wasn't your fault."

Paige snorted softly. "I don't think I can blame Melinda for all this."

"I wasn't talking about blaming Melinda. You could tell your people you were kidnapped or something."

For an instant, Paige could only gasp at the word he'd used. *Kidnapped?*

"That's not even funny," she said when she could find her voice.

"I think it could be a real scream." She flinched when Brian's voice came from only about a foot away. Somehow he had crept from the passenger seat to the back.

"No." She struggled to keep her voice flat. "I don't think it's funny at all. My dad would have a heart attack if he thought I was in danger, and it'd create all kinds of problems for the others—"

A hand clapped across her mouth, cutting off the rest of her words. For a split second she couldn't believe what was happening, then instinct kicked in. She bit down on the fleshy part of a finger near her lips, but though Brian yelled, he didn't let her go. Another hand clamped around the back of her neck, and something heavy—probably his leg—landed across her lap, pinning her to the floor.

The van filled with noise—Melinda's screams, Brian's curses, and Sean's yells. Paige tried to wriggle out of Brian's grasp, but the guy was heavier and much stronger, plus she had nowhere to go.

"Melinda," Sean barked from behind the wheel, "you crawl into the passenger seat, now. Brian, hang on— I've got some duct tape right here."

"What are you *doing*?" Melinda shrieked.

"Shut up and move up here."

Paige drew a deep breath and screamed, but by the time her voice passed Brian's heavy grip, she sounded more like a strangled kitten than a healthy teenage girl. An instant later Brian slapped a piece of duct tape over her mouth. She lifted her hands to yank it away, but he caught her arms and held them together, his fingers closing around her wrists like a vise.

"I need another piece of tape, about a foot long," Brian called, ignoring Paige's muffled protests. "That'll hold her hands. Now what about her feet?"

Sean seemed to think a moment. "Yeah, better safe than sorry, I guess. Let's get her tied up and quiet, then we can make the call."

Paige trembled as Brian pressed her palms together, then wrapped duct tape around her wrists. A moment later she heard tearing sounds, then felt the pressure of his hand on one of her legs. She screamed and kicked against the wall, but one vicious snarl from Brian left her reeling. Her eyes filled with tears, and the voices of the people in the van seemed to fade. She heard Melinda crying in the distance, saying they couldn't do this terrible thing, but Brian and Sean only laughed at her.

"But you're scaring her!"

"She woulda belted me if she could. She's a wildcat!"

Where had that girl found these awful guys?

Paige drew a deep breath and struggled to accept the fact that she was stuck.

And she had no clue what to do.

Through a fog of pain, she felt Brian pull her ankles together, followed by pressure from the duct tape as he wrapped it around her jeans. A moment later he ripped the tape and slapped the final piece to her ankle.

"Okay," he said, a note of finality in his voice. "Pull over on one of those side streets, Sean, wherever you can find a place to park. Let's make the call now."

Lying on the musty blanket, Paige blinked tears from her eyes and tried to listen. She heard the tiny beeps of the phone and knew the call would go through this time. They were dialing the number she had given them earlier—Shane's phone.

She heard other sounds, too . . . the muffled thump of distant drums and the steady rise and fall of a siren. A few blocks away, the Macy's Thanksgiving Day Parade had begun . . . without her.

13

Shane felt his pulse begin to pound with the drums when Bob Stiller raised his head through the trapdoor opening and announced that they'd be moving out soon. "The parade's begun," he said simply. "We'll have to pull out in about ten minutes."

Shane looked around, searching the pedestrians on the street for a sign of his sister. Paige had never been late for a performance, never!

So where in the world was she?

He looked around the float as if she might magically appear, then he caught Liane's eye. No longer accusing, Liane looked frightened . . . and he didn't blame her.

He jumped when the phone in his pocket began to ring. He reached for it, then glanced at the caller ID—this was a stranger calling, not his dad, but it might be someone with news of Paige.

He flipped the phone open. "Hello?"

"Yeah? Who's this?"

"Shane. Who's this?"

"Oh, just call me a fan." The guy on the other end laughed, but a sharpness in his laughter tightened Shane's nerves. "Listen, are you missing someone from your group?"

"Yeah, we are." Grinning, Shane caught Liane's eye and gave her a thumbs-up. "My sister."

"Well, don't you worry about her. We have her right here."

"Thank goodness." Shane exhaled deeply, then nodded at Noah, who had stepped out of position to listen to Shane's half of the conversation. "We've been worried sick about her. Can you take her to one of the parade's security people? They've been looking for her, and they'll bring her right to our float."

"Hold on a minute, bud." The guy on the other end laughed again. "Don't be in such a hurry. You see, here in New York we have a reward system. If you lose something—a dog, a cat, maybe a wallet—you have to offer a reward to get it back. When the finder brings the missing item, the loser rewards him generously and then goes about his business."

Shane looked toward the trapdoor, where Taz had appeared and was listening intently.

"Let me get this straight—you want us to give you a reward for bringing Paige back?"

"Well, thanks, that's very generous of you to offer.

And considering her value, we were thinking a reward of a cool mil might be nice."

"Excuse me—a what?"

"A million dollars, big brother. You know—a one followed by six zeroes."

For a moment Shane was sure his ears were playing tricks on him. One million dollars? For helping a lost girl find her way? This guy was crazy!

Or was he?

"Listen." Shane struggled to remain calm. "We appreciate you finding my sister, but I really don't have time to discuss rewards right now. If you'll take her to a security guard, I'll have our manager contact you after the parade. Leave your name and address with Paige, and we'll make sure you are generously rewarded. I'm not sure about the one million dollars—"

"You'd better *get* sure about it," the guy answered, his voice clipped. "That's the price. One million dollars if you want your girl back."

Turning away, Shane pounded his forehead with his fist. Oh, man. Why'd this have to happen today? He could handle a missing microphone, a few loose wires . . . but he couldn't handle a kidnapping. He could hardly believe this was happening, and he had no idea how to deal with it.

"I don't think you want to do this," he said, finding his voice. "What you're asking sounds more like a kidnapper's demand than—"

"We didn't kidnap her," the guy replied. "She came

with us willingly. We found her, she gave us your number, we'd love to give her back to you. But we need a reward, and times are tough, so we need a good one. I figure you guys have money to burn, so what's a measly million going to matter? That's pocket change to bigwigs like you."

Shane felt his stomach drop to his knees. What did cops and FBI guys always do on TV? They always made sure the demand was for real. They always asked to speak to the missing person.

His voice sounded small in his own ears when he asked, "I'd like to speak to Paige, please."

"She's here, but she can't talk right now," the guy answered. "But I know she wants to hook up with you guys as soon as she can. So talk to whoever you need to talk to, and check on the money. You have our number—you call us when it's all set up."

The line clicked; the phone went silent. Shane lowered it slowly, then looked from Taz to Liane to Noah.

"That was about Paige." He stared at the phone. "Some guy has her, and he won't bring her back unless we give him a million dollars. He wants me to call him back and tell him where he can pick up the money."

"Oh, man." Josiah's face went pale.

Shane looked at Taz. "What do I do?"

Taz jerked his head in a sharp nod, then pointed to the phone in Shane's hand. "You keep that line open while I radio your dad and the police. I don't know what kind of mess Paige is in, but those people don't have a clue who they're messin' with."

Before disappearing into the cab, Taz caught Shane's gaze. "Hang in there, bro. Ride the float, sing your songs, do your thing. We'll get through this, I promise we will."

Shane nodded, but his brain felt numb. Oh, for sure *they'd* get through it—but would Paige?

14

Paige strained to loosen the tape holding her wrists and ankles, then groaned. She knew firsthand the properties of duct tape; Taz used it to fix everything from fraying cords to ripped suitcases. The only way she'd get free is if someone cut her loose . . . or if she could find the frayed end and manage to pull it free—never an easy thing with sticky duct tape.

She lowered her face to the smelly blanket as her eyes began to water. The throb at the back of her head was sending a slow pulse of pain through her skull. She'd lost her glasses—probably when she fell and hit her head— and she had to be a pitiful sight.

"Ohhhhhh, I'm so sorry." Melinda had traded places with Brian, but even though she sat next to Paige, her ragged whisper barely reached Paige's ear. "I didn't know this would happen. Honestly. He's just caught up in the parade, you know, and the crowds. That, and the fact that he and Brian are always looking for a way to make a fast buck—"

Paige turned her head, not wanting Melinda to see her tears, but apparently she wasn't quick enough.

A heavy silence filled the van, then Melinda drew a deep breath. "Hey," Melinda said, her voice sharper now. "You guys have got to let me take the tape off her mouth. She's crying. If her nose gets all runny, she's not going to be able to breathe."

"She'll be fine," Sean snapped.

"Come on." Melinda softened her tone. "She won't scream, will you, Paige?"

Slowly, Paige lifted her head. What good would screaming do now? Practically everyone in New York City was at the parade, listening as groups like YB2 and the Summerville High School band filled the air with ear-shattering music.

She shook her head.

"See there?" Melinda said. "She won't scream. So I'm going to take off the tape, okay?"

"Wait a minute." Paige heard the front seat creak as one of the guys—probably Sean—turned. "If you do scream, Paige, we'll tape you tighter than ever, you hear? You understand what I'm sayin'?"

Paige nodded again. A moment later she inhaled the pungent scent of Melinda's rose perfume and felt the touch of the girl's fingers on her cheek. "I wish I knew an easier way to do this," she said, "but I think quicker is better, okay? I'm just going to rip it off."

Paige tried to squeal a protest, but not in time. Melinda jerked the strip of tape from Paige's mouth, taking with it what felt like three layers of skin. Paige cried out in pain, then snapped her mouth shut.

She curled up in the back, as far from Melinda as she could slide, and rested her head on the cool metal of the door. She licked her lips, felt the sting of raw skin, then drew a deep breath through her mouth.

"Melinda," she whispered, "do you have a tissue?"

"Oh, yeah—let me look in my purse." Melinda scrambled away while Paige lifted her arms and tried to wipe her wet cheeks with her sleeves.

"Hey, Paige," Brian called.

She didn't answer.

"This brother of yours—is he really in charge of the group?"

Paige closed her eyes as a wave of bad feelings swept over her. Shane was never going to forgive her for this. He'd been so proud of being the program director today—boy, had she managed to ruin his plans.

"Cat got your tongue?" Brian called again.

"He's in charge of the group today," Paige answered, keeping her voice level.

"So are you sure he's the one we should be talking to? 'Cause I don't want to waste time with your brother if it's your dad we should be calling. I'm sure your brother is a nice guy and all, but I don't know if he knows how to get the reward money together."

"My brother will speak to my father," she said, turning her head toward the guys up front. "Don't worry about it. If Shane said he'd call, he'll call."

"He'd better call soon," Sean answered. "'Cause since we just stumbled over finding you, you gotta understand that we don't have any way to keep you, if you know what I mean. You'll be too hot to handle by the time the parade is over, so we've got to be rid of you by then."

"Here's a tissue."

Paige listened to the sound of shuffling as the girl crawled closer.

"Um . . . how do you want to do this?"

"Just give it to me." Paige held up her bound wrists, then felt Melinda slide crumpled tissue between her fingers.

"Do you, um, need me to hold it to your nose?"

Paige shook her head. "I can blow my own nose."

And as she did, she decided that she wouldn't cry anymore. These people had frustrated and frightened her spitless, but they were nothing but a trio of idiots. She would not cry anymore, she would not sit and wait to be rescued. If she could stumble into a kidnapping, maybe, with a little help, she could stumble out of one.

She leaned toward Melinda with the tissue in her fingertips. "Help me." She pitched her voice just above a breath. "Help me get out of here."

"Oh." Melinda matched her tone. "I couldn't." The girl

dug through her purse, noisily dropping things onto the floor to cover the sounds of her whisper. "You don't know Brian—he can be mean. He's rough. He beat up his last girlfriend once."

"Hey!"

Paige flinched as Sean yelled from the front seat.

"What are you doing, Mel?"

"Just trying to find her a fresh tissue," Melinda answered. Her voice faded as she gathered up her belongings and dropped them back into her purse. "Can't I help the girl blow her nose? I think you need to be nice to her. It's not going to look good if she tells everybody that you guys were rough with her. You might have a million bucks, but if everybody thinks you were mean—"

"She ain't going to be telling anybody anything," Sean answered, and his words strummed a shiver from Paige's spine.

What did he mean by *that*?

15

Shane soon discovered that a four-foot circle was not large enough to contain his nervous energy. Every particle of his body wanted to jump, to run, to *scream* and do something about Paige's kidnapping, but he had to confine himself to the circle of solid flooring beneath him and wait. And wave. And sing.

To make matters worse, they had entered the parade route. As the "Big Apple" float pushed past the steel barricades at the beginning of the parade route, Shane leaned against the metal support at his back and waved to the throng standing along the steel fence. Thousands cheered as the float inched onto the parade route, and Shane's facial muscles clenched as he strained to smile.

These happy, laughing people had no idea what had happened to YB2—some of them scarcely seemed to notice that Paige was missing.

Paige

While waving, Shane turned and caught Liane's glance. She was waving, too, though her smile was about one-quarter its usual brilliance and her gestures were anything but lively.

When her eyes caught his, her brows lowered in a frown. "I can't believe you're doing this," she said, speaking through her clenched teeth. "Making us go on out here while Paige is missing."

"It wasn't my decision," he answered, smiling at the crowd on Liane's side of the float. "It's what RC and the police said we should do. We have to go ahead like everything's normal."

Movement caught Shane's eye; he turned to see the trapdoor lifting as Taz's head appeared in the opening. "For you," he said, offering a radio to Shane. "RC wants to speak to you."

Grateful for an opportunity to do something, Shane left his position and knelt to accept the radio. He pressed the transmit button. "Dad? You want us to pull out?"

"No." RC's voice sounded worn and ragged as it came over the radio. "The police have been alerted, and they want us to proceed. They don't think this is a professional setup. But the rest of you have to stay together, okay? Look alive, look sharp, don't let anything rattle you. They're sending a detective to stay with you, and he's going to want to look at your phone. You still have that number in memory?"

Shane pulled his cell phone from his pocket. The

phone number from his last received call still glimmered in the window.

"Yeah, I've got their number."

"Good. Give your phone to the police detective when he arrives. He's going to call them and pretend to be you." RC hesitated, and for a moment Shane felt a wave of sympathy for his father, helpless on the other side of Manhattan. "It's going to be okay, Shane. Don't worry."

"I know it will, Dad."

"Okay. Tell Taz to start the musical set. Liane can sing Paige's solo, and Josiah can cover for you at any point if you're talking to the police. Tell Taz to crank up the sync track when needed and you'll be okay."

From where he stood in the cab, Taz nodded. "Roger that."

Shane handed the radio back to Taz, then stood and moved back to his position. As the lively introduction to one of their new songs, "Go Vertical," boomed through the speakers, Liane cast him a questioning look over her shoulder.

"You sing Paige's part," he mouthed, then he looked to Josiah. "And you cover for me if I'm busy."

Josiah nodded as Liane whirled into action. Shane had to hand it to her—when she stepped up to sing Paige's solo, she did it with style and grace. Few of the people in the cheering, clapping crowd would realize that the girl who had created that vocal lick had run into some very messed up people.

"Shane Clawson?"

Startled, Shane looked down at the pavement, where a young bearded man in a heavy denim jacket came jogging up to the float. The man reached into his jacket and pulled out a wallet, then flashed a badge and a shiny police officer's shield.

"I'm Detective Josh Clinton, city police." He tucked his wallet back into his jacket as he slowed to a walk. "I hear you have a phone for me?"

"I do." Shane pulled his cell phone from his pocket. "Be right there."

The athletic cop braced his hands on the top of the float, then pulled himself up. Ignoring the perfect tufts of plastic flowers, he sat down and let his blue-jeaned legs dangle over the edge.

With Shane kneeling beside him, the detective pulled a slim radio from his pocket and called in the number, then he turned the radio down and looked at Shane.

"I'm going to dial this number on your phone and pretend to be you," he said, his voice firm. "Did you speak to them very long the first time?"

Shane raked his hand through his hair. "Um . . . I'm not sure. It was so crazy, you know?"

The cop's mouth curved in a wry smile. "It doesn't matter. I know what you sound like, so I'll try to give them a reasonable imitation."

Shane nodded. He hated to admit it, but at this point he was ready for someone else to take charge.

The detective highlighted the number, then pressed the Send key and held the phone to his ear. Behind

Shane, Noah, Liane, and Josiah were singing their hearts out, but a few of the fans on the street wore puzzled looks. When a group only has five members, Shane supposed, people would notice when only three showed up to perform.

He glanced back at the detective, who still hadn't spoken. Why weren't these people answering the phone?

16

The flat sound of a cell phone cut through the noise in the van. One of the guys turned off the radio, then Sean spoke. "That's gotta be them, man. Answer it."

"You answer it! You're the one who talked to them the first time."

"Yeah, but if I answer it, you gotta go pick up the money. I can't be doing all the work for only a third of the cash."

Paige sat perfectly still as the phone continued to ring. Hard to believe that a case of last-minute jitters could unnerve them now.

Finally, Brian picked up the phone. He grunted a few times, then said, "No, man. You don't need to talk to her."

Shane—or whoever was calling—must have said something convincing, because after a minute Paige heard Brian's seat creak as he turned.

"Hand her the phone," he told Melinda, "but keep your ear next to hers. I want to know what they're saying."

Paige breathed in the scent of Melinda's rosy perfume again as the girl brought the phone to her ear. She drew a deep breath. "Hello?"

"Paige? Are you okay, honey?"

Paige froze. This voice sounded nice, but it wasn't Shane's.

"Yes." She spoke in a guarded tone.

"They haven't hurt you?"

She thought of the cut on her scalp, but this was no time to complain. "I'm okay."

"Good. Is someone there listening?"

Whoever this guy was, he was smart.

"Yeah."

"Fine, then. Give the phone back to whoever's in charge, and don't you worry. We'll have you back in no time."

Paige closed her eyes as Melinda took the phone away. *Thank you, God,* she silently prayed. Shane had found someone to help.

"Yeah?" Brian barked into the phone. "You got our money?"

He waited a minute, then Sean interrupted. "What's he saying? Come on, tell me!"

"He says—" Brian's voice dripped with bitterness— "that they can't get the million dollars, it's too much too soon. But they say they can swing five hundred thousand. They can get that much pretty quick."

Sean began to beat out a rhythm on the steering wheel. Paige's heart pounded with the rhythm for a minute, then relaxed a little when he said, "Okay. There's a parade viewing area with lots of bleachers at Columbus Circle, right near the southwest entrance to Central Park. You tell them to place the money in a leather briefcase. You tell them to get somebody—I don't care who it is, as long as it's not a cop—to leave the briefcase by the light pole at the corner of the park as the YB2 float approaches. Tell 'em if they do that, they'll get their girl back pretty quick. If they don't, they won't. We're gonna make sure our guy gets away in the crowd, then we'll turn the girl loose."

"You got all that?" Brian asked. "You put the five hundred K into a briefcase and leave it at the light pole as the YB2 float comes by—whaddya mean, there's not enough time? You *make* time, bud! So get off the phone and get busy!"

Paige felt her heart sink as Brian snapped the phone closed. As long as somebody had been on the other end, she had felt connected, knowing she wasn't alone in this mess . . . but she wasn't alone, not really. Her entire YB2 family was only a few blocks away, and she knew they were worrying and praying and doing everything they could to get her back.

But could they do enough . . . soon enough?

17

Shane watched as the detective disconnected the call. "They've agreed to take five hundred thousand," Josh Clinton said, keeping his voice pitched beneath the pounding music. "And your father has arranged to have the money ready—now we need to make sure we can have it at the drop point when they want it."

"Why? Where's the drop point?"

"Only a few blocks away, at the first viewing stand."

That didn't sound good. "Oh, man."

A small smile crossed the detective's face. "Don't worry, man, we can always slow the parade down." He pulled his radio from his jacket and turned up the volume. A hiss of static spat in the air, then the detective murmured into the receiver.

"What's our ETA to the Columbus Circle area?"

Someone at the other end squawked back: "Twenty minutes."

"Can we get a man into position with the case? The drop has to be made at the light pole on the southwest corner."

"Um, roger that . . . but the girl's father says he wants to carry it. If they bring the girl, he wants to be there."

Shane felt his stomach tighten as the cop took a deep, frustrated breath. "Can't you talk him out of that idea?"

"Negative. He insists."

"Okay—it's his money. But be sure you have him there on time."

The cop turned the radio down and dropped it back into his coat pocket, then hopped off the float. "Wait," Shane called, kneeling at the edge. "Are you leaving?"

"No," the cop looked up, "I'm staying with you until this thing wraps up. But I look a lot less noticeable down here, don't you think?"

Shane had to admit the man had a point. On the street, the cop looked like an ordinary guy who had somehow managed to slip through one of the police barricades. Atop the YB2 float, he looked . . . well, really out of place.

"So . . ." Shane spread his hands. "What do I do?"

The man gestured toward the others, who were singing "Y B Alone?"

"You do your thing, man, and sing. The more natural

you guys look, the better this entire thing will go down. These guys definitely aren't professionals—they sound like young punks who found your sister and decided to cash in on her celebrity. If we keep things as normal as possible, everything will be fine."

Shane stood on shaky legs and turned to face the crowd, hoping the detective was right.

18

"Okay, man, get ready. You've only got a few minutes to cover a lot of ground."

Paige turned toward the front of the van, which had filled with the sounds of zipping and shuffling.

"Why do I have to make the pickup?" Brian said, a sour note in his voice. "If they nab me, man, I'm dead meat."

"They're not going to nab you as long as I have the girl. That's part of the deal. You just slip through the crowd, run under the bleachers, take advantage of the noise. Nobody's going to touch you, but if they do . . . well, I still have the girl."

Something in the tone of Sean's voice spooked Paige worse than anything she'd heard before.

"Listen, you guys." She turned her face toward the place where Melinda sat. "I don't think you really want to do this. Nothing has happened yet, so if you let me go we can forget any of this ever happened. But if you go out there and pick up a suitcase full of money, you'll be kidnappers—"

"Not kidnappers," Brian argued. "Finders keepers, that's all we're doing."

"Look, Sean—" Paige turned toward the guy who seemed to be in charge—"it's okay. I haven't seen your faces. I don't know what kind of car you're driving or what color it is. I don't have your license plate. So if you let me go, there'll be no way they can track you—I doubt if they'll even try. But if you keep going, there's no way the cops are going to let you escape."

"And what are you going to do?" Sean asked in a snide, singsongy voice. "Just stumble out of here and let yourself get run over in the street?"

"Let me go and I'll find someone and tell them I'm lost," Paige said. "Easy. No big deal. Even if I were to tell anybody everything, I couldn't tell them enough for them to find you."

"No." Sean's voice was flat. "We're in this for the reward and we're going to get it. Too bad your dad marked you down like some kind of blue-light special, but that's okay—we can use five hundred grand. You won't even miss it—you guys are so crazy rich it's disgraceful."

"Please." Having run out of suggestions, Paige waved her hands. "Please, just let me go."

Brian snorted. "Listen, girl, we're doing you a favor. There are all kinds of weirdos out there, and we're keeping you safe. Your old man ought to thank us for keeping you safe in the big city."

Paige bit her lip. She wouldn't cry again, especially not when they were looking at her. She'd tried to reason with them, she'd tried to convince them being nice was the right thing to do.

"Okay," she said simply. "Keep me here and get your money. I'll be quiet. But do me a favor, okay? Loosen this tape around my legs because my feet are going to sleep. I don't have good circulation and if you keep me tied up like this, my feet are going to be too numb to walk by the time I stand up."

"Melinda," Sean said, "shut her up, will you? You'll have to keep her quiet while we figure out the best way to get Brian to Columbus Circle."

Paige felt her heart begin to pound as she heard Melinda move closer. "No," she whispered, "please don't tape my mouth. You've got to help me."

"Hush," Melinda answered, moving so close her perfume threatened to choke Paige's nostrils. Paige heard the stretch of tape, followed by a ripping sound.

But Melinda did not put the tape on Paige's mouth.

"I'm going to lift the edge of the tape at your feet," Melinda whispered. "If you curl up, you'll be able to work at it while I keep the guys busy in front. And when you're back with your family, I want you to tell them I helped you. And I didn't mean to get you into this mess."

Paige stilled as the meaning of Melinda's words hit home. She was helping!

"Thanks." Paige scarcely breathed the word. A moment later she felt Melinda's hands upon her ankles, then heard the steady sound of tape being peeled away.

"Okay," Melinda called brightly, turning toward the front. "She'll be quiet. So—show me which way you're planning to go, Brian. I think you should go out along west Fifty-seventh Street."

As the group up front began to argue about directions and plans, Paige brought her folded knees to her chest, then allowed her hands to drop to her ankles. After a moment her fingers found the loose end of tape and she began to pull, timing her tugs to blend in with the argument that kept exploding from the front seat.

19

Shane kept a smile on his face as he sang, though he felt like doing *anything* but singing. He suspected the others felt the same way, for even though they were singing their hearts out, no one, not even Liane, seemed to sizzle with the usual energy they put into a concert.

Hopefully, no one on the street would notice. The sync track, a vocal recording designed to bolster sound in unpredictable situations, played their voices loud and strong. The singers on the track had smiles in their voices—and why not? On that September day in the studio, the most stressful things they'd had on their minds were learning new music and wondering what Aunt Rhonda had ordered for lunch.

Still singing, Shane glanced down at the ground, where Taz's face was barely visible through a crack beneath the uplifted trapdoor. Taz was talking to someone on the radio—who? Shane felt fear begin to gnaw at his insides. If the cops had bad news, RC might ask them to call Taz, not Shane. He'd want to protect Shane . . . even though Shane was *supposed* to be in charge.

Though he hated to admit it, a part of him was relieved to see Taz handling the radio. Taz was older . . . and Paige wasn't his sister so he wasn't as attached. If bad news came, he'd be more likely to keep his cool.

The undercover detective still walked beside the float, his hands in his pockets, his eyes scanning the crowd from beneath the brim of his Yankees cap. A couple of the navy-coated Macy's employees drifted past on occasion, and Shane felt the corner of his mouth droop when he remembered what he'd been told—the Macy's minders were there to lend a helping hand. Nothing could go wrong when you had your Macy's minder around.

What a bunch of baloney. One Macy's minder hadn't been able to walk a single teenage girl from the hotel to Central Park.

"Hey, Shane! We love you!"

The sound of his name brought Shane out of his thoughts. He had been singing without thinking, now he found himself looking at a pair of little girls who couldn't be more than ten years old.

Catching a breath, he blew them a kiss; the crowd cheered. They were all having a great time. The folks behind the fence-like barricades seemed not to notice the cop, the Macy's staff, or even the open trapdoor where

Taz rode like a disembodied head. They were all too busy screaming for YB2.

Couldn't they see that a huge part of YB2 was missing?

"Go Vertical," he sang with the others,
"Lifting up my life to you.
Go Vertical—
Raising up my voice in praise
Every single prayer I pray is a miracle
Go Vertical."

They finished "Go Vertical" with their arms extended toward the sky, paused for a full five seconds in their choreographed positions, then Shane yelled "Cut" at the top of his lungs. The singers lowered their hands and stepped back to their supports, waving to the cheering crowd as they moved.

Shane let his eyes rove over the mob as he waved. Several teenagers along the front carried posters with his name, Josiah's, and Noah's. Occasionally he caught a glimpse of a sign with a greeting for Paige or Liane, but not many.

He drew in a deep breath as he turned to wave and scope out another section of the crowd. He wasn't sure what he was looking for—on TV and in movies, the kidnappers always stood out. They wore dark clothes, had scruffy beards, and usually had zits or bad skin. But as far as he could see, one person looked pretty much like another. Through a sea of mittened hands and faces buried beneath caps and scarves and high fur collars he saw no sign of Paige. No neon letters pointing to genuine bad guys. No signs that said, "Paige Clawson is being held," along with an address.

Shane saw nothing but a grungy-looking cop in tennis shoes and a Macy's man in a navy coat, and the Macy's guy probably didn't have a clue as to what had happened.

Oh, God, please. Shane closed his eyes in a silent, heartfelt prayer. *How could you lose a girl? Please keep Paige safe, wherever she is, and bring her back to us. Soon.*

20

Paige tugged at the last of the tape around her
ankles as the trio at the front of the van argued about
the best route to the drop-off point.

"Man," Brian said as Melinda and Sean argued about
whether it'd be faster to walk down Columbus or Amsterdam, "what are you gonna do with the money?"

Melinda and Sean stopped bickering.

"What?" Melinda spoke in a sharp voice. "You can't
be serious."

"Serious as a heart attack." A dreamy note had
entered Brian's voice. "It's our reward for keeping the
girl safe, after all. I'm thinking of buying a boat . . .
or maybe a car."

Sean laughed. "Didn't your mom ever tell you not
to count your chickens before they're hatched? First help

me figure out the best way to the drop point. When we have the money, you can plan all you want."

Paige turned away, not wanting to hear any more of their foolish plans. She jerked off the last bit of tape, then cautiously spread her ankles and braced them against the side of the van. Okay—so now she could run if she got out of the van. But how could she find the latch on the door, open it, and slip out without anyone noticing?

She turned her head toward her captors at the front of the vehicle, then brought her legs back into their tucked position.

"Hello," she called, pleased that her voice sounded strong. "I can hardly breathe back here."

"Hey!" Brian's voice sharpened. "Mel, I thought I told you to tape her mouth shut."

"She's been quiet," Melinda answered. "She's not bothering anybody."

"Not yet," Paige answered, "but it's stuffy and it stinks back here."

Melinda cleared her throat. "Um . . . I could go crack the door."

"No way," Sean snapped. "No way on earth are we cracking the door."

Paige bit her lip, then felt her heart sink when Melinda didn't argue. For someone who kept saying she wanted to help, she sure didn't stick her neck out very far.

"Why not open the door?" Paige yelled above their

arguments. "I'm tied up, I can't go anywhere. But if I have to breathe this stink much longer, I'm going to puke all over the place."

"Good grief!" A loud slam echoed throughout the van, and even Paige could tell that Sean had smacked his fist into something. "Go on, Melinda, crack the door for the princess back there. But if her royal highness complains about one more thing, the tape goes back on her mouth, you hear?"

Paige ducked and pretended to cower as Melinda clunked her way through the back of the van. A moment later Paige felt the pressure of her arms as Melinda leaned over her.

"I'm going to undo the latch and leave the door open a bit," Melinda said, speaking in a low voice. "We're in an alley, so we ought to be able to get a little bit of breeze in here."

"Melinda," Paige barely whispered the words, "when you go back up front, turn on the radio, okay?"

"What are you two whispering about back there?" Sean called.

"I didn't say nothin'." Melinda pushed the door open, and Paige felt a wave of fresh air cross her face. "You're hearin' things, Sean."

Just in case Sean had turned to watch them, Paige slumped against the wall of the van, taking care to keep her ankles together as if they were still bound. She didn't know what Sean could see from where he sat, but she was wearing a long skirt over her jeans. If Sean looked at her feet and saw nothing but skirt, chances were good he would believe she still had tape around her ankles . . .

Melinda grumbled as she crawled back up to the front of the van. "You guys are always yellin' at me, tellin' me what to do. From now on, you can get back there and do things yourself."

The guys lowered their voices to a mumble, then Paige heard static from the radio.

"Who told you to turn that on?" Brian asked.

"Nobody. But if you guys are going to sit there and argue, I'm going to listen to some music." She let out a laugh that sounded strained. "Who knows? Maybe I'll hear some YB2."

Brian snorted. "Very funny."

"Forget it." Sean exhaled loudly. "So . . . if you leave now, you should be down Amsterdam in, what? Ten minutes?"

"I'm still not sure I should be the one to go," Brian argued. "This was all your idea. Maybe you should go while I stay here with the van. And you can go to a pay phone and call once you're all clear, and I'll let the girl go when I hear from you."

"I'm not so sure that will work . . . how do we know they won't have a tail on me or some kind of tracking device in the bag?"

"That's why you go someplace safe to check things out. And don't worry—they won't get too close as long as we have the girl."

Paige closed her eyes as her heart began to sink.

These losers didn't have a clue what they were doing . . . and the longer they messed around, the less likely she'd be rescued quickly.

She was going to have to act. And soon.

21

Shane waved until he thought his arm would fall off. The parade had been moving forward at a steady pace, but for about the last five minutes they'd been halted in the same spot. Taz said that a marching band at the beginning of the parade had stopped to perform a routine at the first viewing area and they should expect to wait a few times.

Shane felt his uneasiness rise as he looked out at the crowd. He didn't like being held in one place, only a few feet from the crowd. Anybody could be out there.

From the trapdoor, Taz whistled for Shane's attention. "You want to run through the set again?"

Shane studied the mob. A good showman would take this opportunity to perform—they'd been presented with a captive audience who would scream and shout and dance even if YB2 broke out in an *a cappella* version of "Do Re Mi."

But he didn't feel like singing. He didn't feel like doing anything but jumping off this stupid float and going in search of his sister.

But how did you begin to search for one girl in a city the size of New York?

"I think you should sing, man," Taz called. "The natives are growing restless."

They were. Now that the float had stopped moving, some of the fans had noticed that YB2 was missing a member.

"Hey," a girl yelled, her arms and legs thrust through the bars of a barricade, "where's Paige?"

The cry began to grow like a wind moving through the crowd.

"Where's the piano player?"

"What'd you do with the other girl?"

"You didn't fire Paige, did you?"

Ignoring the questions, Shane waved at pretend faces in the windows of a nearby skyscraper. "Hey," he called over his shoulder, "everybody change places. Give them somebody new to yell at."

Liane and Josiah and Noah gave him doubtful looks, but each of them left their circle and moved to another position. Shane moved to Liane's circle near the giant hockey puck at the back of the float. If something happened—if he saw some suspicious person start to run through the crowd—he wanted to be off this float and giving chase in two seconds flat.

He frowned, though, when he realized he'd moved

away from the detective. The cop was now walking next to Noah . . . and Shane wasn't about to give up his link to the police. The cop—and the phone in his hand—was Shane's only connection to his sister.

"Noah," he called, abandoning the hockey puck, "trade places with me, okay?"

Noah's smile faded as he walked over. "Make up your mind, dude."

"Hey—I'm doing the best I can." Shane reached for the support post as the float lurched forward and began to move again.

He flinched as a phone chirped, and the detective pulled the cell from his pocket. Josh answered, then listened intently for a moment before snapping the phone off.

Forgetting about the crowd, Shane knelt at the edge of the float. "Was that about Paige?"

The detective gave him a grim smile. "We traced the cellular number they left when they called your phone—this guy who has your sister is not very bright. His name is Sean Miller, he's nineteen years old, and he lives in Queens. He's got a rap sheet as long as my arm, but he's never been busted for anything like kidnapping. They're going to get a photo over to us."

"A picture?" Shane looked out at the crowd, where any of the young men in parkas and hats might be Sean Miller.

"So we'll know him when he picks up the money," Detective Clinton replied.

"We're going to pay the ransom?"

"Your dad didn't even hesitate."

Shane didn't speak, but looked at his own cell phone in the cop's hand. He never thought he'd be so anxious to talk to his sister—life with her at home and on the bus usually seemed too close for comfort—but he missed her now.

"I was thinking." He gestured to his phone. "I know you guys know the way to do this and all, but don't you think we should call again? We haven't heard anything from them in a while, and Paige has got to be freaking out."

The cop cast Shane a quick, searching look. "We don't usually call once the drop-off has been established."

"Yeah, okay. But I'd really like to know Paige is okay."

The detective considered for a moment, then his eyes met Shane's. "You know I have to make the call. I spoke to them last; they'll know my voice."

"That's fine."

The cop gave Shane another intent look. "I'll have to clear this with my lieutenant. They won't like me calling without their say-so."

Shane nodded. "Go on, ask him."

He held his breath as the detective pulled out his radio. If they were allowed to call again, would the kidnappers even answer, or were they on their way to pick up the money?

22

Beneath the covering noise of the radio, Paige
edged toward the stream of fresh air coming from the
open door at the back of the van. She couldn't see what
the others were doing, but she imagined Melinda hanging
between the two front seats, blocking Sean's and Brian's
view of the back . . . at least, that's what she *hoped*
Melinda was doing.

She had found the opening and was letting her feet
dangle outside when a radio announcer broke into a
Britney Spears song. "Hey, this story just in," he said,
a note of excitement in his voice. "YB2 singer Paige
Clawson, who had been scheduled to join her band today
during the Macy's Thanksgiving Day Parade, has apparently been abducted. Police say they think her captors
are holding her somewhere in the vicinity of Central

Park, so city residents are asked to keep an eye out for anything suspicious."

"Is anybody even listening?" one of the other deejays broke in. "I thought everybody in Manhattan was down at the parade."

"Not everybody." The other morning deejay maintained his serious tone. "Anyone in the area of Central Park has been asked to keep a lookout for three young adults, ages sixteen to twenty-one. They have been identified as Sean Miller, Melinda Grant, and Brian Weston, all of Queens."

Melinda squeaked. "How can they know that? Oh, man, we are so dead. How did they get our names, Sean? You said nothing was going to happen to us."

"Shut up, Melinda, and let me think."

Paige froze as the volume increased—one of the boys must have turned it up. "Paige Clawson, who is blind, was last seen in the company of Melinda Grant," the deejay continued. "So if you see anything suspicious, please call the New York City police as soon as possible."

Someone snapped off the radio, then Brian groaned. A moment of silence filled the van, then someone thumped something. "I've got it." Sean's voice was calm and confident. "They traced my cell phone, see? We should have thought of that, but it's no big deal. If the cops show up at our house tomorrow, we just tell them I lost my phone in the parade crowd. Some other guys found it, and they used it when they took the girl."

"But . . ." Melinda's voice broke. "But everybody knows we're dating, Sean."

"Not anymore, we're not. I don't know you. I won't know you for a long time, until all the heat has died down."

Even from where she sat, Paige could hear Melinda's sob. The wonderful boyfriend had turned out to be not-so-wonderful.

"Are you sure that'll work?" Brian sounded doubtful. "That sounds lame to me, man."

"No, it'll work. The phone is mine, but I'll toss it in this alley before we leave and some bum will pick it up before long. Let them frame him for this."

"That's a stupid idea." Brian's voice was harder now, and sharp.

"Why is it stupid?"

"Because that girl is hearing every word you say. And when we let her go, she'll tell the cops they had it right in the first place. So we'll never get a chance to spend the money—they'll show up on our doorsteps and cart us away before we even get a chance to smell the cash. They'll put us in prison for life, man. You don't do small time for stuff like this."

"What stuff like this?" Melinda sounded as if she were about to burst into tears. "Come on, you guys, you said this was no big deal. You said it was finders keepers and the money was only a reward for our help in getting her back—"

"Well, it's not that anymore, okay?"

Paige winced at the nasty sound of Sean's voice. "This is some serious stuff, and we have to play our cards right. That means we have to watch our mouths and our steps, and we have to . . ."

His voice dropped to a whisper that not even Paige's sensitive hearing could pick up. But she knew. In her heart, she knew what Sean had decided.

He wanted the money, which meant he could never let her go back to her family. He might not be a killer, but he couldn't afford to let her walk away.

So . . . what would he do to her?

She froze. Any minute they would be looking to the back of the van, wondering how to carry out their plan, and she'd better be in the same position they'd left her in.

As silently as she could, Paige drew her feet back into the van, brought her ankles together, and once again assumed the pose of a bound captive. She wasn't sure how far the door gaped open—she hadn't pushed it too far—but if the wind blew it further open they might realize she had been seconds from slipping out and running away.

And that's exactly what she would do, the minute they started to argue again. She would gather her courage, slide forward, swing her feet to the ground and run as if the devil himself were chasing her. She might run into a wall, a person, or a cop, but nothing could be as bad as remaining here with these guys.

"We can call Chuck," Sean said, his voice low. "He knows how to get rid of . . . problems. He'll know what to do with her."

"He'll want cash," Brian answered. "Maybe not all of it, but he'll want a lot."

"Then let him ask her daddy for the money. He only gave us half, remember? He can give Chuck the other half of the million we asked for."

Paige drew in a deep breath, tightened her muscles, and leaned forward, ready to run . . . and felt her nerve go cold when the cell phone began to ring.

23

Shane found it difficult to wait calmly while Detective Clinton talked on the phone. "Hey," he heard the cop saying, "I want to talk to my sister."

The person on the other end had to be arguing, because the detective toughened his voice. "Whaddya mean? Do you hear singing? I can't sing because I'm worried about Paige. Now let me talk to her now, or nobody's getting anything for you. No money, no nothing. You got that?"

A moment later Clinton handed the phone to Shane.

"Paige?" He frowned as a series of thumps and scratchy sounds came over the line. "Paige, are you there?"

"Shane?"

He closed his eyes. That was Paige's voice, and she sounded okay—nervous, but okay. "You doin' all right?"

"Yeah. And I'm so sorry for all this mess."

"It's not your fault, Paige."

"Yeah . . . it kinda is. But I'll tell you about that later. Are you . . . is somebody coming to get me?"

"Everything is being taken care of." He heard more scratching sounds and whispers, and when Paige spoke again, a tone of annoyance had entered her voice. "They want me to tell you the cops have it all wrong. We heard the report on the radio, so they want me to tell you they found this cell phone on the street."

Shane snorted. "You're kidding. They expect us to believe that?"

Paige managed a laugh, then lowered her voice. "They aren't the brightest bulbs in the pack."

The detective made a hurry-up motion, then whispered: "Tell them we'll be at the drop point in about ten minutes. Are they prepared to meet us?"

Shane heard more scratching noises, then a male voice growled over the line. "You got the money comin'?"

Without a word, Shane handed the phone to the detective, then mouthed the words: *He wants to know about the money.*

Without missing a beat, the detective said, "We'll be at the drop point in ten minutes. If you don't have a man there, you'd better make tracks."

Shane couldn't hear the response, but after a moment the detective disconnected the call.

Shane stared at the phone. "Isn't there some way you can trace where a cell phone call is coming from? I mean, couldn't you have a SWAT team track down the signal or something?"

A look of humor filled the cop's eyes. "You watch a lot of television, kid?"

"Well . . . some."

Detective Clinton shook his head. "If this were a prolonged case and the FBI were involved, maybe we could do some of that high-tech surveillance stuff. But the creeps who are holding your sister aren't criminal masterminds, they're common thugs. They've put this operation on a fast track, and we're confident we can handle it. Besides," he lowered his voice, "look around you. Today more than seven hundred city cops are working on some detail associated with this parade, and at the moment we don't have a lot of extra hands. But we're going to get your sister—I'm confident of that."

Shane didn't answer. He wished he could share the detective's confidence, but he'd seen too many TV shows where the bad guys got away when one thing after another went wrong.

His dad had to be going crazy. And Aunt Rhonda, if she knew. And Mom, if Aunt Rhonda had called her.

But even though they might be worried, Dad and Aunt Rhonda would be praying. And they wouldn't stop until Paige was safe and back where she belonged.

The knowledge of sure and certain prayers didn't bring Paige back, but it did make Shane feel a little better.

24

In the back of the van, Paige listened as the guys' voices grew louder and more nervous. Brian kept arguing that he didn't see why he had to be the one to pick up the money, but Sean kept telling him to go, stay hidden in the crowd, keep an eye out for cops, and be sure to look back to see that no one was following him.

"Here," Melinda said, "wear this hat. If the cops have your name, they probably have your picture, too. The least you can do is wear this hat so they won't see you coming a mile off."

"Nobody's going to see anything in this crowd," Sean answered, his voice tighter than ever.

Paige lifted her hand to her head, where she'd worn Melinda's floppy hat earlier. It must have fallen off in the van a long time ago, but it seemed odd that something once used to disguise Paige would now be used to disguise one of her abductors.

She didn't dare move as the front passenger door opened and closed. She heard the sounds of steps on gravel outside, then a slight cough from outside the open back door.

Good grief, if Brian saw the door open this far he'd know she'd been about to run away! Would he close and lock the door? Would he tell Sean to drive her to Queens or wherever this Chuck guy lived?

"Wait," Sean called, then his door slammed, too. Paige stained to listen, trying to pinpoint their voices, then realized they had moved to the passenger side of the van. Any moment one of them would walk away and the other would climb back in the front seat.

If she was going to move, she had to move *now*. Gulping a quick breath, Paige pushed her feet into the open space beyond the back door, felt asphalt beneath the soles of her shoes, then dropped to the ground behind the van. Without making a sound, she pressed her arms to her sides and rolled beneath the vehicle.

She stopped moving when she felt the pressure of the tires at her head and feet. She must be exactly beneath the back axle, she figured, though she'd never examined an axle and had no idea what one looked like. All she knew was that when Shane went through his model-car-building phase, he was always gluing tires to axles, and the tires would prevent these guys from seeing her if they happened to glance at the ground. She had slipped out so silently that none of them could have heard anything but the sound of their own urgent voices . . . but what, if anything, had Melinda seen?

Paige lay on the cold ground, not moving, as pebbles and gravel bit into the back of her head. Sean and Brian were still arguing about who should make the pickup, then one of them came around to the back of the van, crunching the gravel as he moved.

"What—she's gone!"

Paige clenched her jaw to keep her teeth from chattering as more footsteps approached.

"You *idiot*! Where'd she go?"

"I don't know! She must have taken off toward the road."

"But her feet were tied."

"Obviously not."

Sean's voice, loud and angry now: "Melinda! How could you be so stupid?"

"I . . . I didn't see anything, Sean. I was looking toward the front, keeping a lookout and listening for another radio report—"

Paige flinched as Sean called his girlfriend a name that would have resulted in a grounding-for-months at the Clawson house. "There's nothing that way—the road's back here! If we don't find her we're done for."

"Wait—how far could a blind girl get?" A note of urgency filled Brian's voice. "Instead of griping about it, let's get busy and find her. You go left at the street, I'll go right. We'll find her, bring her back, and take her to Queens. Chuck can handle her after that."

"What about the money?"

"Melinda will pick up the money."

"Me?" Melinda sounded as if she were about to cry. "Oh, no, I'm staying out of it. I can't pick up anything."

An oily tone entered Sean's voice. "It'll work, baby. The cops won't be expecting you. Besides, you know the area better than we do. Just run down there, grab the briefcase, and get to the subway. We'll meet you back at your place later today."

"But what . . . what if they stop me?"

"No big deal. Tell them if they don't let you go, the girl is never comin' back."

Paige held her breath as footsteps came closer, then the van creaked as someone leaned inside. The axle— or whatever it was—lowered, touching the tip of Paige's nose.

"Mel," Sean said, his voice a low growl that made Paige cringe even more than before, "you have to do this. Now be a good girl and do as you're told. Get to the viewing stand, pick up the briefcase, and walk away. Keep your head down and act like you're out for a walk in the park."

"But, Sean, I can't—"

No sound at all from Sean, but another frightened squeak from Melinda. Paige bit her lip. What sort of guy was this, and why in the world would anyone fall for him? She hadn't heard him say anything threatening, but he must have frightened Melinda somehow to make her whimper like that.

"Okay," Melinda whispered, the sound of tears in her voice. "I'll go."

"That's it, man." Sean's voice again, probably speaking to Brian. "Let's hit the street and find her."

A moment later Paige heard the sound of footsteps moving rapidly toward the road. In the distance she heard the rhythmic thump of a marching band's bass drum, accompanied by an occasional bleat of a trumpet.

Carefully, she bent her shoulders and kicked with her feet, shimmying over the ground as she pushed herself forward, toward the front of the vehicle.

She winced as gravel shifted beneath her clothes. Could Melinda hear the sound? She might figure out where Paige was hiding . . . or she might think a rat was scurrying along the alley.

Paige paused when she heard the sound of soft sobs coming from inside the van. Melinda was crying, but why? Did she feel sorry for Paige or for herself?

Something in Paige's heart went out to Melinda, but she wouldn't—she couldn't—allow pity to get the best of her now. Melinda was wishy-washy, trying to please everyone, and she'd already betrayed Paige once.

Paige wouldn't let her do it again.

Still weeping softly, Melinda stepped from the van, blew her nose, then walked swiftly toward the street. Paige turned her head toward the sound of her steps. Where was Melinda going? Was she running away from

Sean and Brian, or was she running toward the parade route and a briefcase filled with half a million dollars of YB2's money?

Paige knew she didn't have time to wonder. No matter where Melinda went, Sean and Brian would spend only a few minutes searching the street. Then they'd hurry back to the van and use it to prowl the area and look for Paige.

Which meant she couldn't walk toward the street—in her blindness, she might walk right into their clutches without realizing what she was doing.

So she had to walk forward, through the alley. She had no idea what lay beyond the van, but she couldn't stay here. When the guys came back and took the van, they'd either expose her or run her over, maybe both.

Using her bent knees to propel herself closer to the front of the van, Paige quietly spat dirt out of her mouth as it showered her from beneath the underside of the van. The cramped space smelled of gasoline and oil and dust. Steeling herself against the scrape of pebbles and asphalt on her leather jacket, she pushed herself forward, inch by inch, until she felt sunlight on her face.

She was free of the vehicle—which meant she was also exposed. So she had to run away from the van, and she had to run quickly. Once she stood up, anyone standing in the opening to the alley would be able to see her.

Brian and Sean would soon be back.

Drawing a deep breath, she sat up, then braced her elbows on the van's bumper and pushed herself upright.

If only she'd had time to chew the tape from her wrists . . . but that could wait. Right now she had to get out of sight.

What did New Yorkers keep in alleys? Cardboard boxes. Maybe trash cans. A few cars, maybe, but probably not small things that could be easily stolen.

She could run until she found some large object, then she could creep around and hide behind it, waiting until her heart stopped pounding. Once she heard the sound of the van moving away, she could take her time and walk through the rest of the alley, following it until she found someone who could lead her back to civilization.

Shivering at the thought of being discovered, Paige flattened herself against the front of the van to orient herself, then leaned forward and launched herself into the alley. She ran as fast as she could, splashing through cold puddles, once nearly slipping on a patch of ice.

Then she smacked against something huge and hard, and the world seemed to clang like a gong. She staggered backward, her ears ringing, and her freezing fingers felt the scaly surface of something metal.

She didn't need her fingers to tell her what her nose had already picked up—she had run headlong into a dumpster—and, judging from the stench, a dumpster in dire need of emptying.

Turning away to gulp in fresh air, Paige felt her way along the side of the trash container, then walked forward until the side bent again. Confident that she now stood on the back side of the smelly garbage bin, she crouched beside it, curling into a ball and sheltering her cold hands in the space between her chest and knees.

"Lord, help," she whispered, her heart pounding hard enough to be heard a yard away. "Lord, please . . . let them come back to the van. And let them leave quickly, without looking around."

As she crouched and waited, half-certain that at any second she'd hear Sean's sour laugh and discover that he'd been standing in front of her the entire time, she found herself thinking back to one of her childhood games. As a little kid, she used to think she could make herself invisible. After all, if she couldn't see people, how could they see her? It wasn't hard to believe herself invisible—once people learned about her blindness they usually stopped talking *to* her and started talking *about* her, as if her brain and tongue and ears had stopped working along with her eyes.

Only after countless games of hide-and-seek with Shane—and realizing that she couldn't hide in plain sight and be truly hidden—had she realized that sighted people had an advantage.

Now she brought her face down and breathed on her freezing fingers, listening for the roar of the van engine. She wasn't sure how long she sat there—fear kept her too frozen to try to check the Braille dial on her watch—but finally she heard arguing voices, the sound of slamming doors, and the start of an engine. The van roared away, squealing its tires as it backed out of the alley.

There was no mistaking Sean and Brian's anger. And who knew where Melinda had gone?

Leaning against the dumpster, Paige pushed herself to a standing position, then felt her shoulders begin to shake. She wanted to break into tears and cry from the sheer relief of having escaped, but she wasn't home yet. She had no idea where she was, her family still thought she was in danger, and Sean and Brian were still out there, probably creeping up and down the street.

So . . . though the street noise was tempting, Paige couldn't walk toward the road. She would have to move further down this alley and hope it would end at another street. One filled with kind people who would protect her and get her home.

She lifted her chin, then turned to her right and began to walk.

25

Shane had known nervousness in his life, but his heart had never hammered like this before. Standing on the float, which had stopped before a gigantic crowd at the first viewing stand, he and the other singers sang "Y B Alone?" and "Go Vertical" while the holiday mob shouted, danced, and cheered.

When the music ended, as Liane and Noah and Josiah waved as though their arms might fall off, Shane peered around the edge of the giant baseball behind him to look for his father at the entrance to Central Park.

Finally, he found him. The police had positioned RC beside a light post and behind a barricade. He stood with his hands in his pockets, looking like a worried father whose child was missing.

Which is exactly what had happened.

The leather briefcase sat on the ground beside RC—

Paige

with plenty of room for someone to wander up, grab it, and take off. The crowd around RC was shifting, not tightly packed like in the viewing stands, but though the crowd moved behind RC, no one had come forward to claim the prize.

Shane's gaze lifted to his father's face. RC's eyes looked determined above his frown, but perspiration glimmered on his forehead—this, despite a chilling wind and a temperature of twenty-something degrees.

The man was obviously worried to death . . . and Shane knew exactly how he felt. Where was their contact? Why hadn't someone come for the ransom?

And what in the world had those creeps done with Paige?

26

Walking at a slow and deliberate pace, Paige stepped through the alley with her arms extended. She didn't want to hit another dumpster—she was pretty sure an egg-sized lump was rising on her forehead—and she didn't want to twist her ankle in a pothole and end up lame in this awful place.

She noticed something as she moved along—the music was not fading, so she definitely wasn't moving away from the parade. But the sound hadn't gotten louder, either, so she probably wasn't moving toward it. She had to be moving parallel to the parade, probably a few blocks west of the north-south route. So all she had to do was reach the end of this alley, turn left, and hope she ran into some kind people in a holiday mood.

A cold wind whistled through the alley, ruffling the hair above her ears. She shivered in her jacket—now that she wasn't running for her life, a coldness had settled upon her bones and her skin. She'd give her weekly allowance for a pair of gloves and earmuffs right now.

She jumped when she stepped on something that crunched like broken glass. Instinctively, she stepped to the right and slid her shoe over the rough ground, hoping she wouldn't step down on some sharp shard that might cut right through the sole of her shoe. She crinkled her nose as a strong odor rose up from the ground—probably alcohol of some kind, strong and nasty.

She took another step to the right, then kept moving, her bound hands extended in case she ran into another obstacle.

As she walked, she thanked God that it was still early in the day. The morning's experience had been nerve-racking, but it would have been ten times worse if she'd been snatched at night. All kinds of dangers came out after dark: rats and roaches and thugs, nasty things that haunted big city alleys when ordinary people were safe in their beds. Of course, she might run into a couple of rats in the daylight, too, but she hoped they'd stay away.

Maybe if she made a little noise, she'd scare them all into their hiding places . . . then again, it probably wasn't a good idea to make too much noise. Sean or Brian might be hiding somewhere in the alley, and they'd grab her before she even knew what had happened.

The wild wind murmured, hooted, and slapped at her cheeks. Paige lifted her arms and tried to rub her face with the sleeves of her jacket. She was going to freeze if she didn't find some shelter soon, and if she didn't get help before dark she'd be in serious trouble.

She wouldn't even consider that possibility. She couldn't think such negative thoughts. She was going to find someone to help her, and then they'd go to the cops, who'd get ahold of RC and the others and tell them not to worry. After that they'd all know they'd been foolish to worry about Paige—she really could take care of herself.

Or could she? Memories of the last few hours rose in her brain. She'd been cocky and arrogant this morning, completely sure she could ditch her escort and handle things on her own, and she'd gotten herself kidnapped as a result. The people who'd snatched her weren't even well-organized . . . they were a pair of jerks and a silly girl who thought they could get away with something.

And they nearly had gotten away with it . . . and they might yet. Because Paige still had no idea where she was and the stupid guys were on their way to steal a fortune from her dad.

"You're the stupid one," she muttered, bringing her arms close as she shivered. "Your pride got you into this, and your pride sure isn't going to get you—"

Her foot struck a hard object, and the force of momentum carried her forward. Too late, Paige threw up her arms, only to discover she had walked into a solid wall.

Her head hit the wall, though not as hard as she'd hit

the dumpster, and she muttered the first word to cross her mind: "Ouch!"

Groaning, she took a half step back and stood in the silence, rubbing her aching forehead with her sleeve. Who would put a brick wall in an alley? Nobody . . . unless it was a wall *across* the alley. Then it probably wasn't a wall, but a building, and she couldn't walk through a building. She was going to have to turn around and retrace every painful step through the broken glass and the smells and the dumpster and the places where rats and roaches might be lurking. Worst of all, by the time she got back to the other end of the alley (where Brian and Sean might still be looking for her), the sounds of the parade would have definitely faded and she'd be further away from rescue than ever.

A low, cackling sound broke the silence. "I've seen blind drunk before—" a voice emerged from the laugher— "but I ain't never seed anybody walk straight into a wall."

Paige stumbled away from the sound, then stepped on something damp and slippery—wet cardboard?

"Watch it, girlie, that's my front porch you're trampin' on."

Paige moved to the side, then lowered her arms and tried to focus on the source of the sound. "Hello? Can you help me? I'm blind, and a pair of guys tried to kidnap me. If you could help me get my hands free and take me to somebody who can call the police—"

"Have you seen George?" the voice asked.

Paige shook her head. "George? I don't know any

George. Besides—I'm blind, like I said, so I can't see any-body."

The woman—if that's what it was—sighed heavily. "I'm blind, too, but mostly in one eye. But if you see George, you tell him to come on back. Tell him Frizzy's waiting for him."

Paige forced a small smile. "Are you Frizzy?"

"George always goes out at dark, but he didn't come home last night. So if you see him, tell him Frizzy's waiting."

Paige sighed. She'd heard about homeless people living in New York, and the other group members had commented on a few they saw lying under street-side cardboard shelters, usually near ventilation vents in the sidewalks. On the drive into Manhattan, Liane had said something about New York being a lot cleaner than it used to be because the mayor had been trying to get the homeless people off the streets.

Maybe he'd only forced them into alleys like this one.

Obviously, this Frizzy was a street person who was not quite right in her thinking. And if she lived in this alley, she might have a knife or something in her pocket . . . which meant she might be able to cut the tape binding Paige's hands. Or she might try to cut Paige.

Paige knew she'd better be careful with this Frizzy person.

Biting her chapped lips, she lifted her face toward the sky. She could still hear the parade, so her family was only a few blocks away, probably close enough to reach within minutes. She could either turn and walk back through the alley in the darkness of her blindness, or she could ask this Frizzy for help.

"Um . . . " Paige turned toward the woman. "I'm Paige."

The woman grunted. "Don't know nothin' about no books."

"No, that's my name. Paige. Are you . . . do they call you Frizzy?"

"You seen George?" The shuffling sounds grew closer, bringing with them the scents of sour milk and body odor—the worst sort of stink Paige had ever inhaled.

With every ounce of her willpower, she resisted the urge to crinkle her nose and turn away. "I haven't seen George," she said gently, "but I'd like to help you look for him. Do you know a way out of this alley, back to the street? Is there a shortcut out of here?"

The woman let out a hacking cough gruffer than any other Paige had heard, then she spat on the ground.

Paige couldn't stop a shudder. "Can you help me?" she asked again.

"Help you what?"

"Help me get out of here. I'm lost, see, and I need to be in a place where there are lots of people. If we go to a place like that, maybe we'll find George."

The old woman spat again. "My feet hurt. I ain't walked much today."

"Well . . . maybe I could help you. You could lean on my arm if you want to."

"I ain't had nothing to eat today, nor yesterday."

Paige swallowed a knot of guilt when she thought about the huge breakfast she'd thrown away in the green-room. "If you help me, I'll get you something to eat. I'll buy you lunch and even dinner if you want."

More shuffling sounds, then a clawlike hand fastened onto Paige's arm. "I used to sleep in the park, you know. But they chased me out a couple of days ago. That's when I lost George. We's been together for nearly two years now."

Paige said nothing, but oddly enough, the woman had begun to make sense. If she and her friend George had lived in the park, the police would have asked them to move on because of preparations for the Thanksgiving parade.

The knot of guilt returned to her throat. Paige was supposed to play a part in that parade, so maybe she had been indirectly responsible for Frizzy's problem.

"Come on," she said softly. "Let's go see if we can find George."

Paige extended her arms again, but tucked her elbows by her side so Frizzy could lean on her right arm as they shuffled toward the street. Frizzy seemed to know which way to go, even with only one good eye, and Paige found herself more than willing to be led.

At that moment, she'd have followed almost anyone who knew their way around New York City.

27

Pivoting in one final twirl at the viewing stand, Shane and the other singers finished the encore to "Y B Alone?" then dropped into a three-count bow. Thunderous applause lifted around them, drowning out the *toot toot* from the high school band marching three slots behind them.

Shane called the final count for the bow, then glanced back at the other singers. Josiah, Noah, and Liane looked as if they'd been wiped out by a marathon concert, but the parade had been the least of their problems.

Liane stepped closer during the break. "I should have stayed with Paige," she muttered beneath a fixed smile as they waved to the crowd. "What was the big deal about going with the Macy's minders? I should have stayed with her, like always. Then we wouldn't have gotten separated."

"You couldn't have known," Shane answered. "Besides, this gig was my responsibility. She's my sister and RC left me in charge. I'm the one who should have watched her—I should have kept all of us in a group. We could have come down in the elevator together, we could have eaten breakfast together in the greenroom, we could have walked as a group to the park—"

"You're being too hard on yourself, dude," Noah interrupted. "Besides, we can't go anywhere in a group these days—we attract too much attention. We had no reason to suspect any of the people from Macy's. It's not your fault—and nobody's blaming you."

Shane gave Noah a weak smile, but he couldn't help blaming himself. Paige was his little sister and he'd felt responsible for her practically since the day she was born. How many times had he been sent out to play with the words "Keep an eye on Paige, Shane—remember, she can't keep up with you"?

Well . . . those words were true today. He hadn't kept an eye on his sister and she hadn't kept up with the group. And somewhere in this monster of a mob there were a couple of people who had no conscience, no morals, no sense of fair play.

His gaze drifted to the place where RC stood by the streetlight, his hands in his pockets, a distracted, desperate look on his face, the briefcase by his side. People moved all around him—people walking behind him on the sidewalk, a couple of folks stepping into the gutter to cut the corner and hurry to the other side of the street—

Wait! The briefcase moved!

Shane pointed to his dad as he yelled at Detective Clinton on the ground. "The briefcase! It's moving!"

As the detective whirled and spoke into his radio, Shane leapt to the street. The cop sprinted toward RC, who blinked and turned to look behind him as if in slow motion. Around RC, the crowd moved and bulged, pressing on the barricades. Shane's shoes had only touched the pavement for a mere instant when the crowd surged through the barricades, toppling them. Screaming fans sprang forward, rushing toward the float like water spilling from a broken dam.

"Shane!" Detective Clinton yelled. "You've got to trust me! Get back on that float!"

Shane took two steps toward the crowd, then realized he had no choice but to obey the detective. If he stayed on the street, he'd either be trampled or stripped of his costume by souvenir seekers . . . and the police who'd been working hard to find Paige would have to stop chasing the kidnappers to protect his brainless body.

"Oh, man!"

Running like a matador before a herd of charging bulls, he sprinted back toward the float, then caught the edge and pushed himself up and over the rim. The fans followed, clambering at the edge of the decorated frame, but none of them had the nerve to climb up after Shane.

"Quick," Noah called to Taz, who was watching from beneath the trapdoor with horror in his brown eyes, "play something!"

An instant later, the encore for "Go Vertical" poured from the speakers. Shane, Noah, Josiah, and Liane hit their marks, then proceeded to sing the chorus with more energy than they'd shown all day.

Somehow, the music worked to soothe the savage mob. The frenzied crowd stopped screaming long enough to sing and clap, and slowly the float began to move away. But as Shane sang, his eyes kept drifting toward the spot where his dad had stood beneath the streetlamp . . . and realized with a sinking heart that his rash action may have caused the police to lose their suspect.

Anyone could have escaped in the horde of fans Shane had accidentally riled. And now they had lost not only Paige, but also a great deal of money . . . and for what?

Absolutely nothing.

Detective Clinton had asked for his trust, but it was hard to trust when your feet were itching to run and your brain was anxious for answers.

28

Paige walked slowly, matching her steps to the old woman's shuffle. Frizzy muttered things that didn't make sense, she smelled like the inside of a mildewed tennis shoe, and her grip felt like that of a cat with untrimmed claws. But she hadn't tried to hurt Paige, she could see where she was going, and she knew the area.

So Paige let herself be led and tried not to inhale too deeply.

"They chased us out of the park," Frizzy was saying, shuffling over the pavement on shoes that sounded as slick as cardboard. "And that's when I lost George. You seen George lately?"

"No, ma'am," Paige answered. "Sorry, but I haven't seen anybody. You know, me being blind and all."

The woman fell silent a moment, then announced, "You got blood on your face."

Paige frowned. Blood? On her face? She must have cut herself when she ran headlong into the dumpster.

"I'm okay," she said, bending slightly to better support Frizzy's weight. "I have a terrible headache, though."

"I haven't seen George today," Frizzy went on. "Have you?"

"No, ma'am. But I can ask someone about him when we get some help. You take us to a place where we can get help, and we'll ask about George when we get there."

"Goin' to get help," Frizzy said, walking on. "I know where to get help."

Paige nodded and let her new friend lead the way. Somehow she felt safer in the company of this old woman.

Paige's heart thumped when she heard the whooshing sounds of cars. They were nearing a street! That could be good and bad—good, because it meant people would be around, and bad, because some of those people could be Sean and Brian. But even Sean and Brian would think twice about grabbing her if they saw her walking with another person. After all, from across the street they wouldn't know Paige was walking with a woman who was crazy as a loon.

"Sure would like a sandwich," Frizzy said, tugging hard on Paige's arm. "Turkey on rye. Lettuce. Maybe some cheese."

Paige nodded. "We could try to get one. I promise, if you get us some help, I'll get you a sandwich. You can have anything on it you want, anything at all."

"Could George have one, too?"

"Sure. The minute we find George, we'll get him a sandwich, too."

"That's good."

Paige smiled. The woman hadn't said anything about her taped wrists; maybe she hadn't even noticed. Or maybe she thought teenage girls *liked* to stumble around with their wrists duct-taped together and their fingers stiff with cold.

The traffic sounds increased, then Paige caught the acrid scent of a diesel engine—probably a city bus rolling past. A moment later she heard the hiss of the bus's brakes as it pulled to a halt somewhere on the street.

"Frizzy!" She would have hugged the woman if her hands had not been tied. "We're back to civilization! Now—can you take us quickly to somebody who can help us? Anybody you see, but try to find someone who looks nice. There are a couple of guys I don't want to ever meet again!"

Paige stepped forward, but Frizzy held on to her arm like dead weight. She wouldn't budge.

"What's wrong?"

The woman resisted Paige's gentle tugging. "I don't like people; people don't like me. They don't like George, neither. I'm not goin' out there."

"But," Paige faltered, "this is the way to get help, see? This is how I can get you a sandwich and how we can find George."

"Not through people." Frizzy turned right and began to walk with a quick step. "Come this way, stay close to the wall. No one sees you if you keep your head down. Blend in with the buildings, that's what I tell George. Mind your own bidness, watch your step, keep your nose to yourself. Don't talk to people."

"But—" Paige raised her head, hoping someone would see her predicament. All around her, she heard the sounds of life—car horns, bus engines, the whistle of a man calling a taxi—but she couldn't tell if anyone was near enough to call for help.

"Come on," Frizzy went on, "this way to help. I know where to get help. It's up here, help for you and me and George."

Paige had no choice but to follow. Surely someone would see her, a rumpled girl with her hands tied, and realize something was terribly wrong.

Any minute now, someone would stop to help her.

29

While the parade proceeded down Broadway, Shane tried to perform his best even though he felt about as energetic as a dirty sock. He caught a glimpse of several famous theaters and read marquees for shows he and Paige had planned to go to—everything he saw seemed to remind him that he'd failed in his responsibility to protect his sister.

The trapdoor opened, and an instant later Taz nodded. "Hey," he called, the radio to his ear. "We've got news!"

Shane stopped waving; so did Liane, Noah, and Josiah. "Yeah?"

"They found the girl from Macy's—they had a tracking device in the briefcase," Taz said. "They're questioning her and she's telling them everything. But she doesn't know where Paige is. She says Paige got away from them in some alley not far from here."

Shane waited, then filled in when Taz didn't answer. "So they're searching for her, right?"

Concentrating on the radio chatter, Taz held up a warning finger, then he lowered the radio and nodded grimly. "They just found the van with the two guys. But there's no sign of Paige."

Shane turned and caught Liane's wide gaze. In her eyes he saw fear, confusion, and frustration. He understood the frustration. He was trying to keep believing Paige was okay, but it sure wasn't easy.

He didn't know what those guys might have done to Paige. And even if she had escaped, she still wasn't safe. The city was a huge, dangerous place for any girl alone, especially one who was blind.

Shane wouldn't relax until his sister was back where she belonged.

30

Paige stumbled as Frizzy led her up wide stone steps. "Frizzy, are we leaving the street? I really think we ought to stay where there are people, someone who could help us find George."

"This is the helping place," Frizzy insisted, hesitating on each step before committing her weight to the next one. "I come here a lot, with George. We get sandwiches."

Paige pressed her chapped lips together. Sandwiches? Maybe there were people here. Frizzy could have led her to a cheap restaurant, maybe a diner, though Paige had never entered a diner with stone steps. But maybe the diner had something special going for Thanksgiving . . . maybe they were offering holiday dinners for the homeless.

Or maybe the kitchen was closed for the holidays and they'd spend a cold afternoon and night huddled outside a locked door.

"Frizzy, are you sure someone's here? It's a holiday, you know."

"I always come here," Frizzy said. "He helps me when I come."

They crossed a stone porch of some sort, then Frizzy shifted her weight. A moment later a bell sounded, an old-fashioned chime that seemed to echo through the building and blow on the wind outside.

This wasn't a diner. You'd walk straight into a diner, and a hostess would be waiting to welcome you.

The sounds of the parade had long faded; Paige heard only the moans of the wind, a few bursts of traffic, and a long, slow creak. A door.

"Frizzy." A man spoke in a gentle voice. "Come in. And do you have a guest?"

"She needs help." Frizzy pulled Paige through the doorway into a warmer space. "Have you seen George?"

Paige hung back, not quite sure if she wanted to leave the open street. For all she knew, this could be the doorway to some hundred-year-old dungeon and this man a torturer of women and puppies.

"I see why she needs help," the man said simply. "It can't be comfortable to have your hands tied up like that."

Paige turned toward him. "No," she said, "it isn't. I was kidnapped."

He made a murmuring sound. "I'd be happy to cut you free."

"Wait." Paige pulled her arms back, not sure she trusted this man. "What I'd really like is the chance to use a telephone."

"We have a phone in the office," the man said. "I can take you there."

Paige hesitated. Frizzy had moved away, but she hadn't gone far—Paige could still smell her.

"What, um, sort of place is this?" she asked.

"I'm sorry," the man said, his voice even more gentle than before. "I didn't realize—you're blind."

"Yes. And I've had a really, really bad morning, and I want to be sure my family knows I'm safe before I do anything else."

"If you come with me, I'll let you use the phone."

Paige took a step back, moving closer to the door. "Can you bring it here?"

The man coughed slightly. "Um . . . I'm afraid our equipment is a bit old-fashioned. But if you'll wait here, perhaps I can find someone with a portable phone. We have some people in the basement who might be able to assist us."

He moved away, his voice echoing in the room, but Paige remained rooted to the spot. The word *basement* had chilled her spine—what was this place and why did they have people in the basement on Thanksgiving? If this were some kind of nightclub or crack house, she wanted out of here, and fast. Sure, they might help Frizzy on occasion—maybe they used her to sell drugs or find runaways to use in their evil crimes.

Paige

She heard shuffling steps, then felt Frizzy's hand on her arm. "You seen George?"

"No," Paige answered, her patience wearing thin. "I haven't seen him. I don't know him."

Frizzy's grip lightened. "I'll go look around. I always find help here. I'll just take a look."

"Frizzy?" Paige felt her uneasiness grow as the woman moved away. Where was she going?

Tracking the sound of those shuffling slippers, Paige followed Frizzy into a room that felt larger, colder, and stonier than the cozy room at the top of the steps. Frizzy kept shuffling along, probably looking for George, and Paige shuffled behind her . . . until she ran into an immovable object and nearly tumbled over it.

With an effort, she righted herself, then ran her hands over the surface. Hey—this was a bench, a wooden bench . . . a pew! Frizzy had led her to a church!

The shuffling sounds had stopped, so Paige felt her way to the edge of the pew, then slipped into a seat and lowered herself to the cushion with a sigh. This felt nothing like their church at home in Orlando. Her church didn't echo, the cushions were soft and deep, the warm pews were always filled with noisy, happy people. The cool atmosphere in their home church was due to the air conditioning, not to the humid chill of a winter street, and the doors that opened to the public were quiet and glass and shiny, not huge wooden things creaking on ancient hinges.

At her home church, the phones were modern and sleek and *definitely* portable.

But what did the differences matter? This was a church, and Frizzy had been right. A lost soul could find help here.

A moment later, the man with the gentle voice approached with soft steps. "Miss?" he asked, "I have a phone for you. Would you . . . would you like me to dial the number?"

An unsteady smile crossed Paige's face. Another man had asked her the same question this morning, but this time she'd have better results.

Smiling, she gave him the number to Shane's cell phone. Her smile deepened when she heard the thin *beep beep* of keys being pressed.

"I brought scissors, too," the man said. He slid the phone between her fingers. "Just in case you'd like to be rid of all that tape around your wrists."

Paige extended her arms. "Thank you. I'd love to be free."

31

Smiling and singing like some sort of programmed automaton, Shane's thoughts kept returning to Paige. Where was she? Was she hurt? Was she frightened?

It was hard to sing about "going vertical" in prayer when his thoughts definitely wanted to remain earthbound with his sister.

Liane was in the middle of Paige's solo when Shane heard the shrill tones of his cell phone from the depths of Detective Clinton's pocket as he walked beside the float.

Breaking every YB2 performance rule, he stopped singing and stared as the policeman lifted the cell phone to his ear, said hello, then broke into a grin.

"Wait a minute," he said, "let me have you speak to your brother. But first tell me where you are." He listened a moment more, then handed the phone to Shane. "She's at St. Jude's, not more than a few blocks northwest of here." He grinned. "We'll send someone to get her right away."

Shane took the phone. "Can I come?"

"I think you need to wait here." The cop gestured to the waiting fans. "We wouldn't want to start a riot, would we?"

Shane pressed the phone to his ear. "Paige?"

"Shane! Are you okay?"

"Us? What about you? We've been worried sick."

"It's okay. I'm at a church, and I'm coming. Don't finish the parade without me!"

32

Paige winced as a pair of fingers gently probed the lump on her forehead with a wet paper towel. "This is a nasty bump," the woman said, sympathy in her voice. "And there's a cut on the back of your head."

"I don't think it's as bad as it looks," Paige said. She didn't want anyone to make a fuss, especially since the others were waiting for her. The last thing she wanted was to be hauled off to some hospital for tests she didn't need.

"Are you sure you don't want someone to take a look at that bump? Head injuries can be serious."

"They can look at it later. I'm fine, I know I am." Paige breathed in the woman's perfume. This woman, unlike Frizzy, smelled of flowers and sweetness. She'd come up from the basement where several church members were preparing a Thanksgiving dinner for anyone who had no place special to go.

The thought of Frizzy sitting downstairs sent a pang of guilt through Paige's soul. "The old woman I came in with—"

Her caring nurse laughed softly. "Frizzy? Everyone around here knows her."

"Do you know what happened to her husband? She keeps asking about him."

"Her husband?"

"Maybe he's her boyfriend."

"Well . . . I don't think Frizzy has a boyfriend. I know she talks kinda crazy sometimes, but if she has a boyfriend, that's news to me."

"Really? 'Cause I'll bet she asked me a dozen times if I knew George, if I'd seen him."

"George?" The woman's voice filled with surprise, then she laughed softly. "Oh, we all know George. And I think you'll be happy to know he's with Frizzy now, down in the basement. Father John fixed them both up with a nice turkey dinner."

Paige sighed, glad to hear Frizzy had been rewarded in some way for all her trouble. Still . . . a hot meal didn't seem like enough. When she and George left this place, they had no place to go but that empty alley.

"Miss Clawson?" The man who had met her at the door—Father John—rapped softly on the door to the ladies' restroom. "If you're feeling okay, your police escort is here."

Paige hopped up from the chair where she'd been sitting. "Thank you for your help." She grasped the woman's hand. "But I need to go. My family has to be worried sick about me."

"I would imagine they are," the woman answered, a smile in her voice.

Paige took Father John's hand and followed him out of the church, then stood with her face lifted to the sunshine. She heard a soft whicker, then an odd scent reached her nose.

She grinned. "Too cool. They sent a mounted police officer?"

"Of course," a man's voice assured her. "We're the fastest way to move around the city today, young lady."

While Father John made a human stirrup with his hands, Paige pulled herself up onto the back of the police officer's saddle.

"Wait!" She tapped his shoulder. "I can't go without Frizzy. She probably saved my life, so I want to do something for her."

Father John's hand fell upon her shoe. "Frizzy may not appreciate what you're offering," he said, his voice calm and understanding. "I'm sure you noticed she's not . . . completely reasonable."

"Then someone should put her into a hospital."

"It's not that easy. There's no money to pay for such things. And she's not willing to go."

Paige shook her head, then squeezed the policeman's arm. It felt strong, dependable . . . like he wasn't the sort of man who would run out on a lady in trouble, even if she did have a name like Frizzy.

"Please." She injected a pleading note into her voice. "Please, can we get her?"

"I can't take her on the horse."

"Can you call for someone else? I really want her to come with me. I want my family to meet her."

She heard the whisper of the police officer's chin against his collar as he nodded. "I'll call someone. But right now I need to get you to your group. I hear they're a few minutes away from the official broadcast area and they're getting antsy."

Slipping her arms around his waist, Paige clung tightly and blinked to stop the tears that had sprung to her eyes.

33

Shane paused from his nonstop waving to look down the road. They had almost reached west Thirty-fourth Street, where they were scheduled to stop in front of the second viewing area—the official broadcast spot—and perform two songs for NBC's cameras. RC had walked ahead to meet them here, and the stands were filled with reporters and photographers.

Would Paige arrive in time?

Shane was turning to look at Liane when his ears picked up the steady *clomp clomp* of a horse approaching on the asphalt. Above the hoofbeats, however, he heard a familiar laugh . . . and realized he was hearing his sister.

"Paige!"

Grinning from ear to ear, she rode up on a horse with a mounted policeman. The police officer helped her dismount, then Detective Clinton boosted her onto the float.

Paige

Cameras flashed, and the crowd along the parade route cheered as if Paige's arrival had all been part of the act.

Helping her to the keyboard in front of the giant baseball bat, Shane paused to grip his sister's hands. Paige had a red lump the size of an egg in the center of her forehead, a scrape on her cheek, and a slightly swollen lip, but otherwise she seemed in good spirits.

"Are you okay?" he shouted above the roaring crowd.

She grinned. "Fine! And tell me—is somebody coming along behind me?"

Surprised, he turned back to the street. Sure enough, another horse was approaching the float, this one occupied by another policeman on a horse . . . and an old woman with frizzy hair, double chins, and some kind of mutt in her arms.

"What in the—"

"She's with me," Paige interrupted, turning toward the horse. "Frizzy! Come up here, okay? You can sit beside me and ride the float. I promise you've never seen New York from this angle!"

A moment later a team of police officers helped the old woman and her dog onto the float. Shane helped Noah guide the strange woman over the floor to Paige's circle, then he tugged on his sister's sleeve.

"Who is that?"

"She helped me." Paige's face was glowing like someone had lit a lantern inside it. "And did you meet George?"

Shane glanced over his shoulder at the police officers, but they had pulled away. "The cop?"

Paige laughed. "No, the dog! He was lost, too, but now he's found. And you know what, Shane?"

Bewildered, he looked at her. "What?"

"It feels *wonderful* to be found!"

Ignoring the cheering crowd, Shane wrapped his sister in the most heartfelt hug he'd given her in years.

34

Safe in her hotel suite, Paige wrapped a towel around her wet hair, then stepped out of the bathroom. Liane was seated at the desk, humming softly to the tune of whatever was playing in her iPod, and through the open doorway, Frizzy was telling George that she had just ordered him a sirloin steak dinner.

Walking into Frizzy's adjoining room, Paige felt her way to an empty bed, then perched on the edge.

"I owe you so much, Frizzy," she said, not knowing if the woman could understand everything she wanted to say. "I've talked to Father John and my dad about some things I could do to help you . . . besides letting you clean up and sleep in a real bed tonight."

The woman didn't answer, but maybe that was a good thing. At least she wasn't asking about George.

"My dad said I could give the reward money to Father

Paige

John's church so they could start a homeless shelter,"
Paige said, "so any time you go back there, you can have
a bed, food, and a shower, if you want it. George can go
with you, too. Father John said it was okay."

Frizzy grunted. "I go there," she said. "I go there
when I need help."

Paige nodded. "When I need help, I go to God, too,"
she said simply. "And I always will."

Go Vertical!

Lord, sometimes I get confused
With all I hear and see
Choices come from every side
They push and pull on me.
Help me to
Look up to you
And in everything I do—

Go Vertical—
Trusting in your plan for me.
Go Vertical—
Always looking for your will
Every single prayer I pray is a miracle
Go Vertical.

There are times when friends want me
To do something that's wrong

Paige

Lord, I need you in my heart
To help me to be strong.
Be my guide
And send your Light
So that all will know that I

Go Vertical—
Trusting in your plan for me.
Go Vertical—
Always looking for your will
Every single prayer I pray is a miracle
Go Vertical.

Come and be
Alive in me
'Cause I want to faithfully

Go Vertical—
Trusting in your plan for me.
Go Vertical—
Always looking for your will
Every single prayer I pray is a miracle
Go Vertical.

Go Vertical—
Lifting up my life to you.
Go Vertical—
Raising up my voice in praise
Every single prayer I pray is a miracle
Go Vertical.

WORDS AND MUSIC BY STEVE SILER, KENT HOOPER, AND HENRY SILER, 2003.

Young Believer™ ON TOUR

Collect all 6 books in the Young Believer on Tour series!

1 **Josiah**

2 **Liane**

3 **Noah**

4 **Paige**

5 **Shane**

6 **Taz**

youngbeliever.com

NEVER STOP BELIEVING!

Have you ever wondered why Christians believe what they do? Or how you're supposed to figure out *what* to believe? Maybe you hear words and phrases and it seems like you're supposed to know what they mean. If you've ever thought about this stuff, then the *Young Believer Bible* is for you! There isn't another Bible like it.

The *Young Believer Bible* will help you understand what the Bible is about, what Christians believe, and how to act on what you've figured out. With dozens of "Can You Believe It?" and "That's a Fact!" notes that tell of the many crazy, miraculous, and hard-to-believe events in the Bible, hundreds of "Say What??" definitions of Christian words you'll hear people talk about, plus many more cool features, you will learn why it's important to . . . **Never stop believing!**

Ready for more?

Other items available in the Young Believer product line:

Young Believer Case Files

Be sure to check out
www.youngbeliever.com

How easy is it to live out your faith?

Sometimes it may seem as though no one is willing to stand up for God today. Well, *Young Believer Case Files* is here to prove that's simply not true!

Meet a group of young believers who had the guts to live out their Christian faith. Some of them had to make tough decisions, others had to hold on to God's promises during sickness or some other loss, and still others found courage to act on what God says is right, even when other people disagreed.

You can have the kind of powerful faith that makes a difference in your own life and in the lives of people around you.

The question is . . . how will YOU live out your faith?

Young Believer 365

Be sure to check out
www.youngbeliever.com

365?? You mean every day??
You'd better believe it!

Maybe you know something about the Bible . . . or maybe you don't. Maybe you know what Christians believe . . . or maybe it's new to you. It's impossible to know everything about the Bible and Christianity because God always has more to show us in his Word. *Young Believer 365* is a great way to learn more about who God is and what he's all about.

Through stories, Scripture verses, and ideas for how to live out your faith, this book will help you grow as a young believer. Experience God's power each day as you learn more about God's amazing love, his awesome plans, and his incredible promises for you.

Start today. See what God has in store for you!

Never stop believing!